RANGER'S BABY

IRON HORSE LEGACY BOOK #2

ELLE JAMES

TWISTED PAGE INC

RANGER'S BABY

IRON HORSE LEGACY BOOK #2

New York Times & *USA Today*
Bestselling Author

ELLE JAMES

EBOOK ISBN: 978-1-62695-259-1

PRINT ISBN: 978-1-62695-266-9

This book is dedicated to my best buddy ever, Chewy. Short for Chewbacca, this little spitfire of a Yorkie melted my heart from the first day I saw him. He's been my shadow, my muse and my best friend. As he grows old, I love him even more. I know some day he will not be with me anymore, and I'll be heartbroken. But I'll have all the good memories of how funny, perky and devoted he was.

Love you, Chewy!
Escape with...
Elle James
aka Myla Jackson

AUTHOR'S NOTE

Enjoy other military books by Elle James

Iron Horse Legacy
Soldier's Duty (#1)
Ranger's Baby (#2)
Marine's Promise (#3)
SEAL's Vow (#4)

Visit ellejames.com for more titles and release dates
For hot cowboys, visit her alter ego Myla Jackson at
mylajackson.com
and join Elle James and Myla Jackson's Newsletter at
Newsletter

CHAPTER 1

FIONA WALKED into the sheriff's office at six in the morning, tired from pulling the night shift.

"Mornin', sunshine," Sheriff Tom Barron called out from where he stood at the station's coffee pot. He set the carafe on the burner and held up his mug. "Need a cup?"

"Yes," she said. "I think that was the longest night ever. Though I'm happy it was a slow night for crime, I would've welcomed a domestic disturbance to help keep me awake."

The sheriff lifted his mug in salute. "I'll pass on domestic disturbances. Last one I handled was at Beau Gaither's place...that worthless piece of—"

She arched an eyebrow. "Now, Tom. You said you were going to cut back on your cursing."

The sheriff ran a hand through his gray hair. "I did, didn't I?" He sighed. "Just the thought of the

Gaither-Faulkner clan gets my blood boiling. One of these days, Beau's going to kill Lindsay. She won't have to press charges. Sadly, she'll be dead."

"Why does she put up with him beating her all the time?"

"Same as everyone else in that family. They're all afraid of Barb, their mama. That woman runs a tight ship of miscreants and takes care of her own, even if it means killing to protect their sorry asses."

Fiona shook her head. "Add breaking and entering and killing to the things she'll do to cover up for her children's indiscretions."

"I'm not gonna lie, I'm a little afraid of her, myself," Tom said. "Until we can get some foolproof evidence on her, I won't touch her with a ten-foot pole."

"Ever find out how that flashlight disappeared out of the evidence locker?" Fiona wondered how the murder weapon could have been lost so completely.

"Not a clue. But I've installed surveillance cameras. That kind of thing won't happen again." He lifted his mug to blow on the steam and take a sip of his coffee. "I hated cutting Mark Faulkner loose. But no evidence— the murder weapon—no conviction."

"Someone needs to shoot that man." Fiona rinsed her mug in the sink and filled it with fragrant brew. "I'd do it myself, if I thought I could get away with it."

The sheriff held up his free hand. "I'd swear on a stack of bibles that it was self-defense. Then again, the way his clan works, they'd make sure you didn't make it to trial. And I'd hate to think of little Caity growing up without her mama. It's hard enough she's growing up without her father. You ever tell him?"

Fiona's lips pressed into a thin line. "Not yet."

"You gonna?"

She nodded. "Soon."

"Caity's how old?"

"You know how old she is." Fiona wished she'd never told him who the father was, but the sheriff was her boss. If anything happened to her, he'd be the one to notify Caity's father.

"Six months after giving birth, and you still haven't told him?" Tom shook his head. "He's in town now, but then I know you're aware of that. What's holding you back?"

"He's not here to see me. He's here because his father's missing. Speaking of which...anything new on James McKinnon's whereabouts?"

Again, the sheriff shook his head. "Nothing."

Fiona nodded, her jaw tight. "I'm counting no news as a good thing. It means we haven't found a body."

"And we haven't found William Reed's killer."

"My bet is when we find the man who murdered Reed, we'll find the McKinnon patriarch." Fiona prayed they found both men alive. James McKinnon was a taciturn father to the McKinnon children, but he was a good man who loved his family, and his family loved him. Fiona had enjoyed a few meals at the McKinnon dinner table growing up. As Duncan McKinnon's best friend and high school study partner, she'd known the McKinnons as well as anyone. She'd been on the hunt for William Reed when James had disappeared.

She'd known then that his disappearance would bring all of the McKinnon boys home to Iron Horse Ranch and her moment of truth would have arrived.

Fiona sipped her coffee, swallowed and stared at the wall in front of her. Why had she waited so long? If she'd thought, after what they'd shared, that he'd come running back to her and declare his love, she'd been sorely disappointed.

To Duncan, she was a friend, nothing more. A friend who'd seduced him one night when he'd had a bit too much to drink.

She could barely forgive herself for taking advantage of him in his inebriated state. But she couldn't regret it. Not now. Not with the results being the most beautiful baby she could have ever dreamed of.

Caity Hannah McKinnon had been born nine months after that fateful night, fifteen months ago. And Duncan McKinnon still didn't know he had a daughter.

Sheriff Barron touched her arm, bringing her back to the present. "Tell him, Fee."

She nodded. "I will."

"In the meantime, you need to get some rest."

She snorted. "That's not likely to happen anytime soon."

"If I could, I'd give you all day shifts, but we're pretty shorthanded as it is."

Fiona shook her head. "You can't play favorites, and no one wants to work graveyard the rest of their lives. Besides, I'm too wound up to sleep right away after getting off duty. I like to spend a few hours with Caity then sleep when she goes down for her nap."

"Ruth is really good about taking her when you need to rest…?"

"She's a life saver. I couldn't do this single parent thing without her."

"You wouldn't have to be a single parent, if you let Caity's daddy know she exists," Tom reminded her.

"I know. I know. I just have to find the right moment to break it to him."

"Fee, there's never a right moment to break it to a man that he has a six-month-old daughter. You'll have to rip off that bandage and make it happen."

He wasn't telling her anything she didn't already know. Nothing was going to make it easier. She'd gone to the airport when he'd been there to pick up his brother. She'd hoped to tell him then. But his family had been all around him, grieving for the loss of their father. The time hadn't been right and never would be.

She'd do it later that evening. After she'd spent

time playing with Caity, and then had a couple hours of fortifying sleep.

The door to the sheriff's office opened, and Ruth Henson entered, carrying the very person Fiona had never imagined she could love more than anyone else in the world.

"Caity, baby." Fiona held out her arms.

Caity blinked and rubbed her eyes before grinning and reaching out her chubby hands to her.

Fiona hugged Caity close, inhaling the baby powder smell of the child and loving her so much her heart felt as if it could burst.

"How's my sweeting?" she cooed. "Did you sleep well for Auntie Ruth?" Looking over Caity's shoulder, Fiona smiled at Ruth.

"She slept from ten until five this morning." Ruth set the diaper bag on the front desk. "Thank you for letting me drop her off here. I have to get to Bozeman for a doctor appointment today. I'll be back this afternoon in time for you to sleep."

"No worries," Fiona said. "I've gone a couple days without sleep before. I can do it again."

The sheriff frowned. "Not and work night shift. Don't you have anyone else who can take Caity while you sleep?"

Fiona thought of Duncan and shoved that thought out of her mind. "Not yet. But hopefully soon."

The sheriff's eyes narrowed, and his eyebrows pulled together. "Think about what I said earlier."

Fiona twisted her mouth into a wry grin. "That's what I meant by *yet*."

Ruth crossed her arms over her chest and frowned at them. "You two are making it really hard for me to eavesdrop and make sense of what you're saying, when I have to stand outside the door to do it."

"It's nothing," Fiona said.

"If nothing means, you don't want to talk about Caity's father, then I get it. You don't want to talk about him. I think it's way past time you told him." She raised her brows. "And since he's in town, there's no time like the present."

Fiona gasped. "You know?"

"I wasn't for certain until a few moments ago. But I am now." Ruth's gray brows rose. "So, what are you waiting for?"

Fiona's gaze switched from Ruth to Tom, and then to Caity. "I don't know what I'm waiting for. Maybe a few hours of sleep?" She gave her baby a crooked smile. "It's only fair that you know your daddy. But I need a few hours of sleep." She faced Ruth again. "I promise to do it tonight. Right after I sleep for at least four hours. I'll need all my strength. He's sure to be angry, and I don't know if I can handle a baby and an angry man all at once."

Ruth's eyes narrowed, "Promise?"

7

Fiona's eyebrows lowered. "I said I would."

With the sheriff and Ruth staring her down with accusing gazes, Fiona knew she wouldn't get out of it. She hiked the diaper bag on her shoulder, hugged Ruth and balanced Caity on her hip. "I'll see you two later."

Fiona left the sheriff's office, tucked Caity into her car seat in the back of her ten-year-old Jeep Wrangler and drove down Main Street in Eagle Rock, turned right onto Glory Road and headed out to the tiny cottage she'd rented, the only place she could afford on a deputy's salary.

The white clapboard house, with its quaint front porch and neat little grass-covered yard, faced Glory Cemetery. Fortunately, it was next door to Ruth's cottage, the one person in all of Eagle Rock who'd made Fiona's life easier throughout her pregnancy and after she'd gone back to work for the sheriff's department. Without Ruth, she didn't know how she would have survived.

As soon as she'd realized she was pregnant, Fiona had known she couldn't continue to live in the apartment she'd rented next to the Blue Moon Tavern. The noise, day and night, would've kept a baby awake and the lack of yard to play in were factors she'd considered when she'd gone house hunting.

Price had been the next biggest deciding factor. When she'd found the little white cottage across from the cemetery, she'd thought at first that it would be a depressing and terrible place to raise a child. Then she'd met Ruth, who'd come out on her porch to say hello with a friendly smile.

Ruth had moved to Eagle Rock a few years before with her husband, when he'd been working for the oil pipeline project running through the area. Her husband had been involved in a terrible accident that had claimed his life.

Instead of moving away, Ruth chose to stay in Eagle Rock in the small cottage they'd shared. She visited him daily in the cemetery, tending the flowers on his grave in the summer and brushing away the snow in the winter.

Ruth's husband was buried two rows over from where Fiona's parents had been laid to rest a few years prior to Ruth's loss.

After talking with Ruth for an hour, Fiona knew the little house on Glory Cemetery Road was the one for her and her unborn child.

Ruth filled the gaping void Fiona's mother had left when she'd passed away right after Fiona had graduated from college with a degree in criminal justice.

As she pulled into the driveway of her cottage, she glanced into the rearview mirror at her daughter, cooing softly and playing with her teething ring. She'd be set for a moment while Fiona unloaded a couple bags of baby clothes Emily Tremont had left for her at the sheriff's station. Emily and Fiona went back to high school days. Emily had been the pretty outgoing friend to Fiona's quiet tomboy shyness.

Fiona had preferred hanging out with Duncan and his brothers rather than playing with makeup and talking about cute boys with Emily. Not until they'd grown and gone away to college and come back had Fiona and Emily forged a lasting, real friendship over coffee and a love of gardening.

Fiona smiled at the roses blooming in her flower beds. She and Emily had found the plants on a trip to Bozeman. Emily said they reminded her of the roses that used to grow in her grandmother's garden in Valier.

Emily was also a thrifty shopper, something Fiona hated doing. She hit the yard sales, thrift stores and sales racks for the beautiful clothing she wore on a daily basis. But she also managed to find the cutest outfits for Caity for dirt cheap. The only real expenses Fiona had for her daughter were keeping her in formula, baby food, diapers and a roof over her head. With the help from Ruth babysitting for next to nothing and Emily finding suitable clothing for a baby, Fiona had been able to take care of her baby, keeping her warm and happy.

"I'll be right back." Fiona gathered the two bags of clothes and carried them up the steps on the front porch.

Shifting one of the bags to her other hand, she reached into her uniform pocket for her key and started to put it into the lock when she realized the door wasn't closed all the way.

Her hackles rose, and she tensed.

Laying the bags on the porch, she shot a glance toward the vehicle, debating whether to edge away from door and return to the sheriff's station, or go in.

She never left the door open. Looking closer, she could see the wooden doorframe was splintered like it had been forced open.

A sound of glass breaking made Fiona draw her service weapon. She nudged the door open and peered inside.

Her heart leaped to her throat. The living room looked as if a tornado had torn through it, upending the furniture, slinging cushions and reducing the tables to kindling.

The sound of more glass breaking set Fiona on edge, and her police training kicked in. She slipped into the living room, carefully placing each foot to avoid making a sound.

Then a darkly clad perp, wearing a ski mask, darted out into the hallway, carrying two of her butcher knives. The whites of his eyes got whiter as he realized he was no longer alone. He flung the knives at her.

Fiona ducked behind a doorway, out of range. The knives clattered to the floor, one sticking into the hardwood.

Footsteps sounded, crunching on glass in the kitchen, and the back door banged open.

Though she wanted to follow and put a bullet through the intruder, Fiona was more afraid he'd circle back and try to take her car.

She ran out the front to where she'd left her car in the cool morning sunlight. She ran to the vehicle and found Caity smiling up at her through the window, completely unaware of the drama unfolding.

A motorcycle roared to life at the back of the house and raced into the woods behind it.

Her hands shaking, Fiona dialed the first person she thought of. As she waited for the line to ring, she told herself over and over, it was the right thing to do.

THE INCESSANT RINGING ripped through Duncan McKinnon's dream, reminding him of the shrill beeping of an alarm warning in the helicopter he and his squad had been traveling in when it had been hit by rocket-propelled grenade fire.

The Black Hawk had been hit badly and plummeted to the ground, the pilot doing his best to land it without killing those souls still alive on board.

They'd landed hard and piled out, dragging the injured away from the fuselage and the ruptured fuel tank. Fire erupted before Duncan could get the co-pilot out of his seat. He burned his hands on the door handle, but finally yanked it open and pulled the man free.

Duncan's hands had been burned and his uniform scorched, but he'd survived the landing. He hadn't realized he had a shrapnel wound until later, after the rescue helicopter arrived to airlift the survivors and the casualties.

"Duncan, honey," a woman's sweet voice called out to him. "Duncan, wake up."

He blinked open his eyes and stared up into his mother's face. For a moment, he didn't recognize her. She didn't fit in the harsh environment of Afghanistan hills. The land of his dreams and nightmares.

When he shifted, he realized he was in a warm, soft bed, not on the hardpacked dirt. "Mom?"

His mother's brow wrinkled as she held out the telephone. "It's Fiona. She says she needs to talk to you. It's an emergency."

Duncan sat up and grabbed the phone. "Fiona?"

"Yeah, it's me." She hesitated. "I need you to come to my place as soon as possible."

"What's wrong?"

"I had a break in," she said.

"Did you call the sheriff?" he asked, throwing aside the sheet as he leaped out of bed.

"I will next," she said. "But I need you to come. We need to talk. It's important, or I wouldn't bother you."

"Fee, you're not bothering me. I'll be there as soon

as I get dressed." He started to hang up, but her voice stopped him.

"I don't live by the Blue Moose anymore."

"Give me the address."

"I live on Glory Road, right across from the cemetery," she said. "I'll be out front when you get here."

"Do I need to bring a gun?" he asked.

"No, I don't think so. Not yet. Hurry."

"I'm on the way." He dropped the phone on the bed and shoved his feet into his jeans, wincing at the pain shooting through his bad leg. The physical therapist and the doctors had told him he'd probably have pain in that leg for the rest of his life. The Army thought the injury was enough to put him before a Medical Review Board. The outcome had yet to be decided.

The trip home, though the reason was dire, had been a welcome respite from sitting in his apartment wondering what was going to happen to him.

Shoving his feet into boots, he grabbed a denim shirt and ran down the stairs.

"Everything all right?" his mother called out.

"I'll let you know," he said and slammed through the front door.

Twenty minutes later, he blew into Eagle Rock, the tail of his truck skidding sideways as he turned onto Glory Road headed for the cemetery.

He saw her standing beside an older model SUV,

wearing her deputy uniform, a worried frown on her face.

His heart thudded hard in his chest as he came to a halt beside her and leaped out of the vehicle.

Fiona stood with her shoulders back, her chin held high and her long, lean body looking totally badass and sexy in her uniform. Though her long auburn hair was pulled back sharply from her face into a tight bun at the base of her neck, he knew how soft, silky and curly it was and how pretty she was when she let it hang down around her creamy white shoulders.

The last time he'd seen her, other than the brief glimpse at the airport when his brother had arrived, he'd had a few drinks with his old friend and ended up in her apartment next to the Blue Moon to sleep it off. Only he hadn't slept it off. He'd stripped her out of that sexy uniform and made love to her.

When he'd woken up sober, she'd been gone, having left for work. And he'd been filled with remorse.

He'd made love with the woman who'd been his best friend since they were in grade school together. And worse, he'd had to leave to return to duty that day. Though he'd driven by the sheriff's department, she hadn't been there. He hadn't had time to track her down, having to get back to the ranch to pack up and get to Bozeman Airport in time to catch his flight back to Ft. Lewis, Washington.

He'd tried calling her, but she hadn't answered. After a couple of weeks, he'd figured she didn't want to talk to him. Of all the stupid things he'd done in his life, making love with Fiona, though it had felt amazing at the time, had been the stupidest. That few minutes of magic had cost him the best friend he'd ever had. And he couldn't forgive himself for that.

Now she stood in front of him, as sexy as the day they'd made love, if not more. Was she just a little curvier? Fiona had always been an athlete, with a long, lean body made for running and hard work. She could sling an eighty-pound bale of hay with the best of them.

He got out of his truck and came around the hood to stand in front of her.

"Hey," she said softly.

Duncan hesitated a split second then grabbed her arms, pulling her into a tight hug. "Hey, yourself." He said, pressing her to him, loving the feel of her against him. "Are you all right?"

She nodded, her forehead leaning against his chest. "I'm sorry I woke you."

"I should have been up already." He set her at arm's length and stared down into her eyes. "What's wrong?"

"Someone broke into my house," she said. "Sheriff Barron is on his way."

"He should have been here already. He's closer than the Iron Horse Ranch."

Fiona stepped back until Duncan was forced to drop his hands from her arms. "I wanted to talk to you first."

"I don't understand."

"I wouldn't have called you, if I didn't think it was important." She turned away from him and opened the back door of the SUV and reached in.

When she straightened, she had a baby in her arms.

Duncan's heart dropped to his belly. "You have a baby? Did you get married in the past year?" The thought of Fiona with another man didn't sit well with him. And the baby was so small. It couldn't be a year old.

"No, I didn't get married in the fifteen months since you left." She turned the baby so that he could see her face.

"Hey, sweetie," he forced himself to say and touched the soft skin of her cheek, regret tugging hard at his heart. This little girl could have been his, had he stuck around. "Too bad she didn't get your red hair. But she's got your green eyes."

"No, she takes after her father. He has brown hair and green eyes." Fiona shook her head, her frown deepening and the corners of her lips quirking upward. "She's six months old, Duncan. Do the math."

He stared at the baby who had dark brown hair and green eyes, his head spinning, his mind unable to grasp what she was saying. An intense feeling of anger toward the man who'd given her a child, blinding him to anything else she might say. "I don't understand."

"It takes nine months to have a baby. She's six months old. That's fifteen months all together."

Duncan couldn't think past Fiona having moved on after they'd made love.

Fiona closed her eyes, inhaled and let it out slowly. "Duncan, meet Caity. Caity, meet Duncan McKinnon...your daddy."

CHAPTER 2

FIONA COULD SEE the moment it hit him. Duncan staggered back a step, his brow descending into a wicked scowl. After an excruciatingly long moment, he spoke, his voice gravelly, "Don't mess with me, Fee."

"I wish I was. I should have told you a long time ago, but I wasn't sure how." She held out Caity. "This is Caity. She's your daughter." Fiona shoved the baby into his hands and moved backward, forcing him to take the child.

"Wait. What do I do with it?" He held Caity out in front of him, his eyes wide.

"You hold her, hug her and love her. She's an incredibly smart and happy baby."

As if to prove her wrong, Caity's bottom lip jutted outward and her face wrinkled.

Duncan's eyes rounded with a look of abject fear. "What's wrong with her?"

"You're scaring her. You need to hold her close. She likes to be held close." *Like I do*, Fiona wanted to add, but bit down hard on her lip to keep the words from coming out.

Duncan pulled the baby close to him and curved his thickly muscled arm around her back. "Like this?"

Quickly, Caity's pouty lip receded, and she stared at the man holding her, her eyes wide. She reached up and grabbed his ear.

Fiona chuckled. "Like that. It's not that difficult. If I could learn, so can you."

"But you've got six months on me," he said.

Fiona swallowed hard at the bile rising up her throat. "I know. And I'm truly sorry I didn't tell you sooner. Again. I didn't know how."

Duncan looked at Caity, shaking his head, his brow furrowing. Then he looked past his daughter to Fiona. "Six months."

"I know." Fiona's heart squeezed hard. "I'm sorry. It shouldn't have happened. You were drunk. I took advantage of you, and then...I didn't want to tie you down. You had your career. I had to deal with the consequences of my rash actions."

Duncan's scowl remained in place. "Consequences? A baby is not just consequences."

Fiona threw her hands in the air and spun away.

How much more could she screw up this conversation? "This isn't how I'd planned to tell you."

"And how did you plan to tell me?"

She shook her head and turned back to him. "I don't know. That's been the problem all along. After you left, I thought…" Her shoulders slumped. "I don't know what I thought."

Caity, apparently sensing the couple's distress, puckered up and let out a resounding wail.

Duncan's frown disappeared, and a look of panic filled his face. "What did I do? Did I hurt her?"

Fiona reached for the baby. "No. You didn't hurt her. She's very sensitive to moods. She knows when I'm angry or sad." She smiled at Caity and bounced her in her arms. "Hey, sweetie pie, it's okay. We're not mad, are we?" She shot a glance at Duncan.

Duncan frowned.

Caity cried louder.

"You're still frowning," Fiona said. "You'll have to do better than that to convince her."

"How am I supposed to do anything else? I just found out I've had a kid for six months. Six months I can't get back."

Caity cried louder.

"Shh, sweetie. He doesn't know how much that upsets you." She kissed Caity's brow. "He's really not all bad. Give him a chance."

Duncan's frown smoothed, and he lowered his voice. "I'm sorry. I'm not sure what I'm supposed to do. It's not every day a man is pulled out of bed on an emergency call only to find out he has a baby."

At the smooth, calming sound of Duncan's deep voice, Caity's wails simmered to sniffles.

"I know," Fiona said. "I'd planned on telling you later this evening, after I'd had a chance to sleep." She turned toward the house. "But I came home to an intruder."

Duncan spun toward the house.

"Don't worry. He's gone." Fiona shifted Caity to her hip. "But he trashed my house."

The sheriff chose that moment to pull up in the driveway and got out.

He held out his hand to Duncan. "Duncan. Good to see you."

Duncan shook the man's hand. "You too, Sheriff."

"I'm sorry to report that we haven't had a single lead on your father's whereabouts."

Duncan's jaw tightened. "I'm sure you're doing everything you can."

The sheriff nodded. "We are. Got the state police working with us, and we're checking into every person we can find who has ever come in contact with Reed."

Duncan nodded. "Thank you."

Sheriff Barron glanced from Duncan to Fiona.

Fiona nodded. "He knows."

Duncan shoved a hand through his short-cropped hair. "You knew?"

The sheriff nodded. "Caity looks like a McKinnon." He chucked the baby beneath the chin. "Don't ya, honey?"

Caity grabbed his finger and giggled.

"But I'm not here to go over that," the sheriff's brow dipped. "What happened here, Guthrie? And why didn't you call me first?" He said, eyeing Duncan then turning toward Fiona's house.

Fiona led them up the steps and stood to the side as Duncan and Sheriff Barron entered the house.

Duncan swore.

Fiona fought to keep from telling him not to swear in front of the baby but figured it wasn't the time. Besides, other than baby babble, Caity hadn't started talking. But she would soon.

Fiona stepped in after the men and stood beside the butcher knife stuck in the wood floor.

"The intruder threw that at you?" Duncan asked.

Fiona nodded. "I'm just glad Caity was in the car. Normally, I walk in with her."

Duncan's face grew hard, his lips thinning into a line. "Did you see who it was?"

She shook her head. "He wore dark clothes, and a ski mask covered his face." She nodded toward the back of the house. "He ran out the back and rode off on what sounded like a motorcycle."

The sheriff and Duncan walked through the house to the kitchen.

Fiona hadn't seen all the damage to her place

because after she'd confronted the man in the ski mask, she'd remained outside with Caity in the vehicle until Duncan had arrived. She hadn't felt comfortable going back inside with Caity without backup, and she hadn't felt right leaving her daughter alone in the vehicle while she inspected the full extent of the damage.

Every drawer in the kitchen had been pulled out and dumped on the floor. Half of the upper cabinets had been emptied onto the floor, including her glasses and dishes. Broken glass and plates littered the floor.

Her heart lurched and sank to the pit of her belly. She hadn't had much to begin with. Now, she had less.

Squaring her shoulders, she waited for the men to enter the small bedrooms.

Duncan walked into Caity's bedroom and swore again. The crib had been dumped on its side, the mattress flung across the floor. Stuffed animals had been decapitated, the stuffing lying in puffs of white.

Caity leaned toward her favorite pink elephant. The arm had been ripped off and an eye was missing, but Fiona scooped it up and handed it to her. "I'll fix it, baby. Don't you worry."

She tried to sound confident, but her voice wobbled, and her eyes stung. Who could be so vicious they'd destroy a baby's room?

When she entered her own bedroom, Fiona

gasped.

Written in bright red spray paint across the gray-blue wall were the words, *Shut up or die.*

Duncan turned toward her and pulled her into his arms, Caity and all. "You can't stay here."

She shook her head. "This is our home. I don't have anywhere else to go."

"You'll come stay at Iron Horse Ranch."

Fiona shook her head. "No. I can't do that."

"If not for yourself, do it for Caity," Duncan insisted. "You can't stay here, just you and Caity. It's too dangerous."

"Ruth lives next door. She takes care of Caity while I work."

"Then she can stay at the ranch as well."

The sheriff turned to Fiona. "Duncan's right. This isn't some random break-in. Whoever hit your home targeted you specifically. And I have a suspicion I know who."

Fiona's teeth clenched, and she nodded. "Me, too."

"The Faulkner Clan," the sheriff stated.

She nodded again.

"Barb Faulkner's bunch?" Duncan asked. "You mean someone hasn't killed them yet?"

The sheriff shook his head. "That bunch has been up to no good for decades. But every time we get something on them, the evidence miraculously disappears, or the witness ends up dead or in a coma."

Duncan stared at Fiona. "Please don't tell me you

witnessed one of them committing a crime."

She grimaced. "I witnessed Mark Faulkner threatening to kill Clay Bennett."

"Clay Bennett?" Duncan frowned. "The former football linebacker, Clay Bennett?"

Fiona nodded. "He was found dumped in a ditch along the highway heading south out of town. He'd died of blunt force trauma."

"Someone had beaten him to death," the sheriff said. "The man had bruises all over his body, and his skull was cracked in several places."

"The first officers on the scene found a heavy-duty flashlight near the body," Fiona said.

The sheriff shook his head. "We had it locked up in the evidence locker, but it went for a walk sometime yesterday. The flashlight was supposed to go to the state crime lab for examination. We're working on how that got misplaced." The sheriff's face was grim. "All I gotta say is heads are gonna roll when I find out who let that cat out of the bag. I have a feeling we were finally close to putting one of those dirtbags out of commission for good."

"Can your testimony about hearing Faulkner threatening Clay be enough to put him in jail?"

Fiona shook her head. "Not without hard evidence. Anyone can say they're going to kill someone. Until we have solid evidence, hearsay won't hold up in court. And we had it, until yesterday, fingerprints and all."

"Surely they know that." Duncan stared up at the writing on the wall. "Then why did they threaten you?"

"The Faulkners haven't always been the sharpest tools in the shed," Sheriff Barron said. "Could be they didn't know the evidence is missing. I'm sure your intruder had orders to threaten you before the flashlight disappeared. He had to have been watching your house and Ruth's next door to know when they were both empty. If the Faulkners knew the murder weapon had gone missing, they might not have thought to cancel the order to terrorize you. Barb's minions carry out their orders or suffer the consequences. She rules the roost with an iron fist."

"Guess I'll be knocking on her door next," Fiona said.

"Not without backup," the sheriff said.

"But you agree, we need to look for who stole the flashlight and for who might be in possession of a can of red spray paint and a black ski mask." Fiona met the sheriff's gaze.

The sheriff frowned. "I really don't want you anywhere near the Faulkners. They might claim you're trespassing on their property and shoot you."

Fiona gave a half-smile. "If you send backup with me, you'll have an eyewitness to murder." She stared down at Caity. "Although, I don't really want to be the bait to put the Faulkners in jail. Caity needs me to come home in one piece."

"Exactly."

Fiona met the sheriff's gaze head-on. "But I'm not the only one in the department with family depending on them to return home alive. You can't treat me any differently than any one of the men on the force."

The sheriff scraped a hand down his wrinkled face. "I knew it was a mistake taking you on as a sheriff's deputy."

"You have to give me the same assignments as the men, Tom."

"The hell he does." Duncan stepped into the conversation. "You have a daughter who has now been threatened along with you. You think that upended baby crib would have ended any differently with a baby in it?" He shook his head. "The fact you've been targeted means Caity has been targeted as well."

The sheriff nodded. "And I'd treat any one of my men the same by saying, you're off this case."

"But we can't let Mark Faulkner get away with murder." Fiona knew they were right, but they had been so close to putting a killer away.

"You're off the case, Guthrie," the sheriff said, his tone firm. "Now, are you going to stay at the Iron Horse Ranch, or do I have to make room for you and the baby in my jailhouse? You're not staying here."

Fiona scowled. "The hell I'm not. I have a gun. I won't let anyone hurt Caity. And that paint can be covered. I don't need anyone to take care of me and Caity. We've been on our own from the beginning, and we've done just fine."

"Then why the hell did you call me, if you didn't want me to get involved?" Duncan squared off with her. "Caity is my baby, too. I'm not leaving her here in this house. If you want to stay…stay. But I'm taking my daughter somewhere safe. And that isn't here."

Duncan plucked Caity out of Fiona's arms and limped toward the door.

"You can't take my baby," she cried and followed him out of the house.

"I damn sure can."

"She's mine."

"And mine." He turned with the baby held close to his chest his big hand covering her back. "I won't have her threatened and not do anything about it. What's the problem, Fiona? It makes no sense that you want me to know about her, but you don't want me to help."

"I do want you to help me protect her," Fiona said. Her voice softened to a whisper. "I just don't want to go to the Iron Horse Ranch."

"Why? Because you'll have to face my mother and siblings when you tell them that they have another member of the family they didn't know about? Are you feeling guilty?" He glared at her. "Well, you should. You robbed us of watching her grow for six months. We won't be left out of her life any longer. Yes, you should feel bad for keeping her from us."

Caity's face puckered and great big tears rolled out of her eyes and down her cheeks.

"You're scaring her." Fiona reached out for her baby.

"You're scaring me," Duncan said and then changed the tone of his voice to something softer. "Caity needs protection. You need it, too. Face the music, Fiona, and let the McKinnons help you."

Fiona fought back the tears threatening to fall from her own eyes. Everything Duncan said was true. Her shoulders sagged. "Your mother and siblings are like family to me. I never wanted to disappoint them."

Duncan smiled at Caity and brushed a tear from her damp cheek. "Well then, don't start now." He said it in a singsong tone without looking at Fiona. "Caity needs her mama to make things right and keep her safe. Don't you, sweetheart?"

Caity grabbed his thumb and held on.

Fiona stared at the two. They looked so much alike it made her chest hurt.

"Just say you'll go," the sheriff urged. "It'll make me feel a whole lot better, knowing you have others around you to look out for you two."

Fiona nodded, swallowed hard at the lump in her throat and said, "Okay. I'll go.

CHAPTER 3

DUNCAN HELD Caity as Fiona picked through the rubble of her home for clothing, diapers, formula and anything else she might need for an extended stay at the Iron Horse Ranch. When she'd finished packing, the sheriff helped her haul everything out to her SUV and packed it into the back.

He would rather have packed everything into his own truck, but Fiona would need her vehicle to get her to and from work.

Not that he liked the idea of her working as a deputy when someone had issued a death threat against her.

The sheriff held her door for her and shut it after she'd climbed in. "I'm putting you on day shift until we get to the bottom of this."

"You can't—"

"I would do the same for any deputy in the

department, so don't play the sex card on me." The sheriff looked through the back window. "And don't report to work for two days. I have to work through the details of the schedule change, and I don't want to worry about you showing up for duty when I don't need you."

Fiona appeared to want to argue the point, but she bit down on her bottom lip and nodded. "Yes, sir."

Duncan let go of the breath he'd been holding. "I'll follow you out to the ranch. You remember the way?"

She nodded. "Like the back of my hand." Fiona shifted into reverse and waited for the other two vehicles to back out before she could get out of the drive and onto the road headed out of town.

Duncan followed close enough to cut off any trouble should it arise.

The entire drive to the ranch, he rolled her announcement over and over in his mind.

He was a daddy.

Those words made his insides quake. He had a daughter. A living, breathing human, totally dependent on him and her mother to keep her safe from harm. The magnitude of the responsibility left him feeling nauseated. How the hell had this happened?

Oh, he knew all about the birds and the bees, but...he was a daddy. He wasn't ready to be a father. He hadn't had nine months to dwell on it, to prepare himself and to think through how he'd raise a child in this crazy world they lived in.

No, he'd had no prior warning, no pre-game coaching, no pre-battle training. He was being launched into it blind and unprepared.

His hands gripped the steering wheel until his knuckles turned white. How was he supposed to be a father to a child when the mother didn't want to be with him? If the Army decided he was fit for duty, he'd be shipped back to Ft. Lewis and deployed to another godforsaken continent to fight battles against people who didn't give a shit that he was a father and had a baby to come home to.

Holy hell. This changed everything. Every damn thing.

By the time they pulled through the stone and wrought iron gate at the Iron Horse Ranch, Duncan was in a full panic. He'd never been panicked before in his life. Hell, going into battle had been less stressful than plunging into fatherhood.

When he drove up next to Fiona and shifted into park, he struggled to pull himself together. One thing he'd learned in his Army career was to never show weakness. Even when you're scared out of your mind. And he was scared out of his mind.

He squared his shoulders and dropped down out of the truck. When he landed on his feet, his bad leg gave, and he would have fallen to his knees had he not been holding onto the door of the truck.

He cursed. How the hell was he going to protect his daughter when he had a bum leg?

Duncan couldn't think about that now. He had to focus on being strong for Caity. She and Fiona needed him to protect them from whoever had trashed their house and written those threatening words on their wall.

Fiona climbed out of the SUV, chewing on her bottom lip. She opened the back door and would have reached into the backseat for Caity, but Duncan beat her to the baby.

"Please," he said. "Let me."

"Are you going to break it to your family?" Fiona asked.

He lifted Caity up into his arms and nodded. "I'll tell them. But I want you by my side."

She nodded. "Deal."

As they started toward the house, his mother stepped out the front door, followed by his sister Molly and his brothers, Angus, Colin and Sebastian.

"Fiona." His mother hurried down the stairs to engulf her in a hug. "It's been so long since you've been out to the ranch. I've missed you."

"I've missed you, too," Fiona said, her voice cracking.

"What was the emergency?" his mother asked, looking from Duncan to Fiona. "Everything all right?"

Fiona looked up at Duncan.

He cleared his throat. "Let's get the baby out of the sun."

The others remained on the porch, waiting for Duncan and Fiona to climb up to them.

Angus stood with his arms crossed over his chest, Colin's brows dipped, and Sebastian stared at them through narrowed eyes.

"Oh, Fiona, I've seen you around town with this sweet little thing and haven't found the time to stop and congratulate you." Molly reached for the baby in Duncan's arms. "Let me have that sweet baby."

Duncan leaned away from his sister. "In a moment. We have something we need to say."

When they were all on the porch, his mother turned with raised eyebrows. "So, what's got your britches in a bunch?" she asked.

Beside him, Fiona choked on a chuckle.

Duncan stood tall and shook his head. "My britches are never in a bunch, Mother."

"No?" Colin said with a sly smile. "You have a strange look on your face."

"Come to think of it, I've never seen you hold a baby before. Maybe that's what's making you look weird," Sebastian said

"Can it," Angus said. "Let the man have his say." He gave Duncan the nod. "Go ahead."

Duncan turned Caity to face his family, suddenly nervous and proud at the same time. "You all remember Fiona, right?

"Of course, we know Fiona. She spent most of her summers here on the ranch riding horses and eating dinner at our table," his mother said.

The others nodded.

"Well," Duncan swallowed. This was harder than he'd expected, giving him a new appreciation for why Fiona had taken so long to tell him about his child. "This is Caity, Fiona's baby girl."

His mother started forward. "Congratulations, Fiona. Caity is beautiful." When she reached for the child, Duncan turned slightly away, keeping his hold on his daughter. "I'm not finished."

Molly clapped a hand over her mouth, her eyes widening. "She's got brown hair and green eyes." She looked from Fiona to Duncan and back to Caity. "She's a McKinnon! She's your baby, too!" Molly jumped up and down, clapping her hands. "I knew it. I knew you two were meant to be together."

Duncan frowned at his sister. "Thanks. I'm glad you held back while I made the announcement," he said, his voice dripping with sarcasm.

"Is she right?" his mother said, her voice light, almost a whisper. "Is Caity yours?" Her gaze locked with Duncan's. "Is she my very first grandchild?"

Duncan saw the wonder in his mother's eyes and any hardness in his heart melted. "Yes, Mother, Caity is mine. And yes, that makes her your first grandchild."

"You're serious?" Angus asked. "This is my niece?"

"Now, that's a helluva wakeup call in the morning," Sebastian smiled. "Congratulations, old man. I never pictured you as being the first to bring Mom a grandbaby."

Duncan nodded. "It's as much a surprise to you all as it was to me. But it's the truth, and I couldn't be happier."

"What the hell?" Colin said, his face splitting into a grin. "When did you have time to come back to Eagle Rock and make a baby?"

Fiona's cheeks reddened.

Duncan slipped his free arm around her. "It happened when I was on leave here fifteen months ago. The night before I left to return to duty and a thirteen-month deployment to Afghanistan."

"And you didn't tell him?" his mother said, her brow dipping.

Fiona reached out for his mother's hands. "It was one night. I didn't know where he was going or how he would feel about it." She bowed her head. "I know I should have told him sooner, but I didn't want him to feel obligated."

Molly reeled back. "Are you kidding? Even if my big dufus of a brother wasn't happy about having a baby, we all would've been happy to help."

"Most of you were off, happy to be in the military. I couldn't lay that on you."

Molly planted her fists on her hips. "But you sure

as heck could have laid it on us. We've been here all this time."

"She's right," his mother said. "We would've gladly helped." She took a big breath and waved a hand. "But that's all water under the bridge. What's important is that we help now. What was the emergency?" She glanced from Fiona to Duncan and back. "Or was telling Duncan he had a child the news?"

Duncan's lips firmed. "Fiona had an intruder in her home. He threw knives at her and left a death threat."

His mother's eyes widened, and she slipped an arm around Fiona. "Oh, dear. I'm so sorry to hear that." Then as only his mother could do, she organized them. "There's no question, then...you and Caity are staying here with us." Her face blossomed into a wide grin. "Which means I have more time with this precious little one. I can't believe I have a grandbaby. Come to Nana, sweet Caity-did." His mother held out her arms.

Duncan didn't want to let go of his daughter, but the look of abject adoration on his mother's face was too much to ignore.

The woman had been through hell with the disappearance of her husband. The joy of a grandchild brought the light back to her countenance and made Duncan have more hope for the future than he'd had less than an hour ago.

Molly was next to hold out her arms. "Mom, let

me hold my niece. I can't believe I'm an aunt!" While she waited her turn to hold the baby, she turned to Fiona. "How was your pregnancy? Did you have a lot of morning sickness? Did you go natural or have a C-section?" She peppered Fiona with questions Duncan didn't understand...but wanted to. He'd missed it all. The pregnancy, feeling the first time his baby kicked, being there for the delivery...

Angus pulled him into a bear hug. "Can't believe my little brother is a father. You sneaky bastard. All these years, I thought you and Fiona were just friends."

"No kidding," Sebastian clapped him hard on the back. "Caity looks like you, poor kid." He winked.

Colin shook his head. "I'm an uncle." He patted his chest as if looking for something. "I feel like I should pass out cigars or something. Do they still do that?"

The women moved inside and laid a blanket on the floor of the living room for Caity to lay on. Duncan's mother and sister sat on the floor on either side of the baby.

"I need to unpack the SUV," Fiona said.

"We'll keep an eye on Caity," Molly offered.

"Absolutely," his mother said. "Let the boys unload."

Duncan shook his head, hesitant to leave the room and the tiny baby that was his. The enormity of his responsibility toward the little girl hit him all over again.

"Come on, old man," Colin said. "Let's get them moved in."

"Where do you want me to put them?" Duncan asked his mother.

"They can have your old room," his mother said. "You can sleep in my sewing room beside them. The sofa in that room folds out into a bed. Oh, and Colin, bring the baby crib down from the attic."

"Baby crib?" Colin asked.

"You heard me." She grinned. "I saved it for just such an occasion as a visit from my future grandchildren. I brought all five of my children home to that bed. And your father wanted me to sell it when Molly outgrew it." She lifted her chin. "He'll be beside himself when he gets home to find a grandchild under his roof." For a moment her eyes got glassy. She blinked, and the moment was gone.

Duncan felt the loss of his father as much as the rest of his siblings, but his mother had been with him the longest. She was the one who had to sleep alone in the bed they'd shared for the past thirty-five years.

He pushed the sadness to the back of his mind and turned to the task at hand.

Fiona walked with him, Sebastian and Angus out to the SUV.

Angus grabbed the portable playpen and carried it inside. Sebastian took the highchair. Duncan carried the swing, and Fiona grabbed a suitcase and a sack of clothes.

Several trips later, they had everything she'd managed to pack inside the house and distributed to where they belonged. The playpen stood in a corner of the living room, but his mother and Molly had yet to tire of entertaining the new member of the family.

Caity had flipped onto her tummy and jerked her arms and legs out to the side.

His mother smiled. "She'll be crawling before you know it. They learn so much in the first year of their lives. You have so many *firsts* to look forward to. Her first time to sit up on her own, her first time to stand. The first time she walks without assistance, her first word…" His mother sighed. "I loved tracking each and every one of your firsts."

Duncan shot a glance toward Fiona. How many of Caity's *firsts* had he already missed?

Based on his mother's list, he hadn't missed too many. But he would have liked to have been there from the beginning, He wondered if his baby would have difficulty bonding with him as her father, since she hadn't been with him for her first few months.

Like his mother had stated, that was water under the bridge. He couldn't get it back, and he couldn't hold a grudge. Not when mother and child were in such close proximity. Caity could sense her mother's moods. If he wanted to bond with his little girl, he had to make peace with her mother.

At the same time, he had to keep them safe from

harm. With Caity staying at the ranch, she'd be safe among his family.

Fiona would be another matter altogether. How was he supposed to keep her safe when she stepped into harm's way every day she worked as a deputy sheriff?

CHAPTER 4

FIONA STARED down at Mrs. McKinnon and Molly playing with Caity and regretted keeping the secret for so long. The McKinnon clan had always been a tight-knit family. Caity would be well loved in their midst. She deserved to know all of her family— grandparents, uncles and aunt. And they deserved to be with the beautiful baby girl who looked so much like them.

Truth was, Fiona felt some of the burden of raising her daughter alone shift off her shoulders. It was at once a scary and a liberating feeling. With both of her parents gone, she'd felt her job left Caity vulnerable.

She'd shared the information about her child's father with Sheriff Barron, with instructions that, if anything happened to her, he was to notify Duncan immediately. If he'd been unable to contact Duncan, he was to go to the McKinnon family and let them take Caity in until such a time as Fiona recovered, if she recovered at all.

Mrs. McKinnon rose from the floor, her gaze remaining on Caity. "I'll be right back, Caity, after I help your mommy get settled."

Then she turned to Fiona and hugged her. "Thank you so much for sharing her with us." She turned toward the staircase with a sigh. "It's been so long since there's been a baby in this house, I don't know how to act."

"You raised five children beautifully," Fiona said. "You're a natural."

Mrs. McKinnon laughed. "I don't know about that. We didn't have a guide book. James was hard on them a lot of the time, but they knew we loved them and only wanted the best for them."

Fiona remembered how the taciturn McKinnon patriarch had scared her with his gruffness, but how he could be so gentle with his wife.

She touched the woman's arm. "We're still looking for him," Fiona assured her.

She gave Fiona a wobbly smile. "I know you're doing the best you can. The house just isn't the same without his booming voice and huge presence."

With a nod, Fiona followed her up the stairs to Duncan's bedroom. She smiled as she entered. It appeared much as it had when he'd been in high school. They'd spent many evenings sitting cross-legged on the bed, going over chemistry and algebra, preparing for tests. She'd helped him with history and English assignments, and he'd helped her with anything to do with math.

A lump formed in her throat.

His mother chuckled as she looked around the room. "We'll have to redecorate this room. It seems to have been frozen in time over a decade ago." She shook her head. "If I had known you two were a thing back then, I wouldn't have let you study in his room unchaperoned."

Fiona snorted. "Trust me, we weren't any more than friends back then. He was the football star with cheerleaders hanging all over him. I was the tomboy who would rather have been out riding than doing my hair." She raised a hand to her slicked back hair. If she let it loose, it framed her face in a mass of riotous, dark red curls. "I'd still rather ride horses than do my hair. I was lucky to have him as a friend."

"Sweetheart, he was lucky to have you. You kept him grounded when the other girls were all about the drama." Mrs. McKinnon smiled gently. "And you were kind enough to go with him to the senior prom when his date called it off at the last minute." She fisted a hand on her hip. "How in the world did you find a dress at such a late date?"

Fiona shrugged. "I guess I got lucky." And boy had she. Her mother had insisted on her attending her prom, even though she didn't have a date. She'd made

Fiona go on a dress shopping expedition that had made her want to tear out her hair. When they'd found a dress they could both live with, Fiona had snatched it up and marched toward the counter, ready to get the hell out of the shop and back outside where she felt more at home.

Sticker shock set in when the clerk rang up her choice. Fiona told the clerk never mind. She wasn't that interested in the dress after all. She'd walked out the door, climbed into the family SUV and waited for her mother, who'd taken an inordinate amount of time telling the clerk she wouldn't be buying the dress.

When her mother came out of the shop carrying a garment bag, Fiona's heart dropped into her belly. Her mother had spent a small fortune on a single dress. Fiona couldn't disappoint her by telling her she didn't feel well and wouldn't be going to the prom after all.

She'd felt like her dress would be her date—until the night before prom, when Duncan called, asking her to go to the prom as his date.

Even so many years later, she could still feel the flutter of her nerves as she'd let her mother apply makeup she never wore. She'd fixed her crazy hair, sweeping it up into a messy bun on the crown of her head. Long tendrils had spiraled down around her ears, driving her insane throughout the night.

But the look Duncan had given her when he'd

arrived to pick her up in his father's shiny black truck had been worth the effort. He'd stared at her as if seeing her for the first time.

Heat had rushed up into her cheeks and down to pool low in her loins. Fiona had always been more than halfway in love with Duncan since she'd sat beside him in the fourth grade.

Seeing him in the rented tuxedo, sporting a tight, white rosebud in his lapel, his hair slicked back and a single dark strand falling over his forehead had made her heart skip beats and butterflies flutter in her belly. That was the night she'd started dreaming about being kissed by the handsome football jock. She'd known she was the replacement date, but she couldn't help fantasizing about the young man and wishing he could see her as more than just a friend. She'd been stuck in the friend zone for so long, she hadn't thought she'd ever pull herself out without damaging that friendship. So, she hadn't.

They'd gone to prom. His friends had all given him hell about his date dumping him the day before, but then stared at her as if they'd never met her.

Duncan had treated her like his date, presenting her with a rose corsage he clumsily pinned to her dress, his knuckles brushing against the swell of her breasts.

That had started her blood thrumming through her veins. Until that moment, she'd been okay with being relegated to the friend zone. After he'd touched her once, she'd known she could never go back. She loved Duncan McKinnon with all of her heart. And she could never tell him. God forbid he insist on marrying the mother of his child, for the sake of Caity.

Deep down, Fiona had hoped Duncan would contact her and profess his love for her rather than be forced into a relationship because of a baby. The real reason she hadn't contacted him was because she'd wanted him to love her as much as she loved him. For herself. Not for Caity. Caity was a bonus, but children only stuck around for eighteen or twenty years. Fiona wanted Duncan for a lifetime.

Mrs. McKinnon helped her set up the crib Colin brought down from the attic. "I'll wash the sheets I had for the mattress. I'm sure they're dusty after decades in storage."

"Thank you for all you're doing for us."

Mrs. McKinnon waved a hand. "I should be thanking you. James and I have been wishing for grandchildren for the past ten years. But none of our offspring seemed to be in a hurry to provide additional McKinnons. I really thought it would be Angus. Now that he and Bree are together, I expect there will be wedding bells soon and babies shortly after." The woman clasped her hands together and smiled. "The cousins will grow up together. It all makes my heart sing." Her smile faded. "James would be beside himself. That big, old gruff demeanor of his hides a teddy bear who loves the babies. He'll be so happy when he comes home."

When.

Fiona's heart squeezed hard inside her chest. Mrs. McKinnon held out hope they'd find her husband alive. After the first forty-eight hours, Fiona figured his chances of resurfacing on his own two feet were getting slimmer by the minute.

Not wanting to squash the woman's optimism, she nodded. "I love that Caity will grow up around her grandparents. I never knew mine."

"Darling," Mrs. McKinnon touched her arm, "your parents were middle-aged when you came along. I was sad to hear when they passed. But don't you worry, we'll shower our little Caity-did with all the grandparent love she can stand."

Fiona nodded, the back of her throat burning from unshed tears.

Mrs. McKinnon started to pull clothes out of the drawers and set them on the bed.

"Wait," Fiona said. "Are those Duncan's?"

Mrs. McKinnon paused with a handful of T-shirts. "Yes, they are."

"Does the room he'll be sleeping in have a dresser and a closet?" Fiona asked.

"No," Mrs. McKinnon said. "But he can live out of his suitcase for now. He might not be here for long."

The thought of Duncan leaving again so so made her heart tighten into a knot. The last tim been to the ranch, he'd only been there for a week. "How long does he have here, this time?"

"He told me he'd stay until James is found." The McKinnon matriarch glanced toward the window. "I don't know if that will happen before he runs out of leave. At the rate we're going, it might take a while."

Fiona selfishly wished Duncan would stay forever. If they weren't meant to be together as a couple, he would at least be close enough to be a part of his daughter's life. Caity would love her father and his family as much as Fiona. And she'd be accepted more readily.

Who couldn't love that cherubic smile?

After they finished changing the sheets on the bed and putting away the clothes Fiona had brought with her, Fiona and Mrs. McKinnon descended to the first floor to find Duncan on his back on the floor, holding Caity above him, his brothers watching, with grins on their faces.

The infant giggled and flapped her arms, a huge smile on her face.

"Look, Fee, she likes to fly," Duncan said. "I'll have you parachuting before you're fifteenth birthday."

Fiona gasped. "Oh, no you will not. She'll keep her feet firmly planted on the ground."

Duncan winked up at Fiona. "Thought that would get your goat." He smiled up at his daughter. "You'll have to wait until you're eighteen to make your own decision."

Seeing him down on the floor with Caity warmed Fiona's heart. Even if he didn't love her, he would come to love his daughter. Already, Caity had a way of wrapping adults around her chubby little fingers.

"You want me to take her?" Fiona asked.

"No, I've got her until she cries."

"Can you hold her still for a moment?" Fiona reached out to touch her daughter's diaper. It felt warm and heavy. "She needs to be changed. Are you up to it?"

Instantly, the smile on his face fell away. "I don't know. What do I do?"

Molly laughed. "This is rich. The football jock, badass Ranger looks a little scared about changing a baby's diaper."

He glared at his sister. "When was the last time you changed a diaper?"

Molly's smile faded. "She wasn't talking about me."

"Yeah, well, until you've changed a diaper, keep your jabs to yourself." He rolled to his feet, holding onto Caity as he came up. He bent to scoop up the diaper bag and set it out the couch. Then he dropped down on the cushion, hooking an arm around Caity's belly. "Come on squirt, it's time your daddy learned how to change a diaper."

Fiona chuckled. "Are you going to wing it? Or do you need help?"

"How hard can this be?"

Fiona grimaced. "You might want to get down on the floor with her the first time. She tends to wiggle a lot."

He frowned. "Okay." Duncan adjusted his position and eased to the floor, wincing when pain shot through his bad leg. He bit back a curse and settled Caity on the rug between his legs. Then he looked for the way into the one-piece outfit she wore.

"There are snaps at the crotch," Fiona said, holding back her laughter. The tough guy who always studied up before his next play was going in blind on this one. And Fiona didn't want to give him too much information. He seemed to want to do it on his own.

He fumbled with the snaps, finally freeing all three, and then pulled the tabs free on the sides of the diaper.

When he drew the diaper down, he leaned back, his face screwing up in horror. "Holy hell, what crawled up in this kid and died?"

Fiona, Mrs. McKinnon, Molly, Angus, Colin and Sebastian all burst out laughing.

Duncan quickly covered Caity with the edge of the diaper and glared at his family. "It's not funny. I think she's sick or something."

Fiona brushed the tears from her eyes and shook her head. "Do you want me to take over? Changing a poopy diaper is hard on even the toughest of us."

"No. She's my daughter. I need to know how to

do this." He dug in the diaper bag for a fresh diaper and the wipes. Pulling out ten or twelve of the wipes, he squared his shoulders, drew in a deep breath and held it while he attacked the situation again.

Fiona caught herself wanting to lean over and help him, but he'd insisted he could do it on his own. So, she held back and let him go for it.

Mrs. McKinnon stood by, biting her lip. Fiona could tell she wanted to say something, but she didn't.

Duncan peeled back the soiled diaper and blinked as if the room had just filled with tear gas.

He started to take the diaper out from under her but stopped when the nasty stuff smeared. "How do you keep it from getting on the floor," he said, his voice strained.

Molly squatted next to him on the floor. "I think you have to hold her up by the ankles with one hand and wipe the stuff off with the other."

Caity laughed and kicked, getting her feet into the mess in the diaper.

"Holy sh—"

"Duncan," his mother warned. "Caity will start talking soon. Don't let her first word be a curse word."

"Grrr," he grumbled and fumbled to capture Caity's legs as she kicked and twisted. "How do you... Come on sweetie. Geez, how can you smell so bad and look so cute at the same time?" He grabbed a heel and grimaced. "Yuck."

His brothers stood way back, laughing.

"Shut up, jerks," he shot back at them as he held onto the two little dirty heels. "Okay, now what do I do?"

"Use the diaper to take off what you can and the wipes to clean the rest," his mother said.

Fiona clapped her hand over her mouth to keep from laughing out loud. She had to give the guy credit for trying.

He managed to clean Caity's bottom, holding her high above the trouble below, practically standing her on her head.

When he'd used at least a dozen wipes, he pulled the messy diaper away and lowered her to the carpet.

"I wouldn't do that," his mother said.

"Do what?"

"Lay her on the floor without a diaper beneath her," his mother said.

At that moment Caity relaxed and grinned. A wet spot spread out beneath her, making a circle on the rug beneath her.

Molly burst out laughing. "Mom was right. She peed."

Duncan's frown deepened. "You're not helping." He grabbed a disposable diaper and struggled to unfold it and lay it out—on a dry patch on the floor.

"I'm going for some towels and rug cleaner," his mother said.

"I'm so sorry," Fiona said.

"Don't be," Mrs. McKinnon said. "I can't tell you how many times I get hit in the face by one of my boys. Caity's nothing compared to them." She winked. "And the entertainment factor was worth it." She hurried away, chuckling.

"Glad I could provide the afternoon's sideshow," Duncan muttered. He finally had the diaper beneath the baby's bottom. In order to pull it up between her legs, he had to let go of the heels he'd just cleaned.

As soon as he did, Caity dug them into the carpet and twisted her torso, flipping onto her tummy.

"Hold still, little one," he said through gritted teeth, "we're almost to the finish line." He rolled her to her back and quickly pulled the diaper up between her legs and applied the tape to hold it in place.

"There. We did it." He lifted Caity up in triumph, The diaper slid down her legs and fell to the floor. "What the hel—"

"Duncan..." his mother said as she reentered the room, carrying towels. "Give me that child. You can practice another time. She'll need to be washed down and changed into a dry outfit now."

Duncan handed Caity to his mother and shot a frown toward Fiona. "I can do this."

She nodded. "It takes practice. I at least had the

pleasure of learning when she was too small to wiggle out of my grip."

Duncan pushed to his feet, wincing. He limped a few steps then crossed to where his mother sat on the couch, starting over with a fresh diaper. She had Caity covered in record time, keeping control of the baby's flailing legs and arms throughout the process. Then she secured the diaper in place, making sure it fit snugly around Caity's middle.

Meanwhile, Molly bent to clean up the puddle on the rug. "Good job, brother," she said.

"I want to see you do better," he said.

"I had the benefit of seeing you do it all wrong and Mom do it right. I think I can handle it."

"Sure, until you have to."

Fiona fished a fresh one-piece outfit out of the diaper bag and handed it to Mrs. McKinnon. The older woman pulled the wet one over the child's head, ran a clean, damp cloth over her body and followed it with a dry hand towel. Then she slipped the clean outfit over her head and down her body, snapping it between her legs.

Mrs. McKinnon sat the baby up on the couch and smiled down at her. "There. Now, you can have your supper."

Caity had found her fist and was sucking on it, making slurping sounds.

"I have formula in the bag," Fiona said. "I'll go mix some now." She fished a plastic bag out of the diaper bag and picked up the soiled diaper with it, tying it securely inside. Then she took out the can of formula powder and a bottle.

"I'll go with you," Molly said. "I need to know how to do these things. I don't want to make a disaster of my first time babysitting like Duncan."

Fiona shot a glance over her shoulder at the man she loved. "He did good for his first time. He'll do even better next time."

Duncan's gaze followed her across the floor and down the hall until she turned into the kitchen. She knew this because when she cast one final look down the hall, he was still watching her.

Heat filled her cheeks, and she ducked into the kitchen, reminding herself the man didn't think of her the same way. He'd only made love to her because he'd had too much to drink and she'd come on to him.

They were friends, that was all.

She drew in a deep breath and let it out. How she wished they could be so much more.

CHAPTER 5

ONCE FIONA WAS out of sight, Duncan dragged his gaze back to the living room and his brothers dropping onto the sofas and chairs scattered around the hardwood floors.

"Yeah," Duncan snorted. "*Now*, you come closer."

Angus shook his head. "I wasn't getting any nearer until you dealt with the smell."

"Just wait," Duncan warned. "Your turn is coming."

Angus frowned. "Bree loves children. I guess, when we get hitched, we'll be popping out a couple of our own."

"You did good on your proposal," Molly said.

"Smart move to do it in front of family." Colin grinned. "She had to say yes."

Molly smiled. "She would have anyway. She's crazy about Angus."

Sebastian shook his head. "I don't know what she sees in him."

Molly ignored her brother's dig, having grown up listening to them poke at each other every chance they got. "Have you set a date?"

Angus shook his head. "We're waiting. I wanted to get married yesterday, but Bree doesn't want to disappoint the mothers. We're waiting to set a date until we know more about Dad."

Duncan nodded. "Probably for the best. Mom needs us to be focused. Some of us only have a few weeks before we return to active duty." The pain in his leg twinged, reminding him that he might not be headed that direction. The sound of voices laughing in the kitchen made him feel that, for the first time since he'd been injured, it might not be all that bad to get out of the military.

With his father missing, his mother needed support. Angus would be there, but the ranch was big enough he could use help running it. Even if—*when*—their father returned, he was getting up there in age and should consider turning over the day-to-day operations to his sons. That had been James McKinnon's plan all along. After his sons served on active duty, he'd expected them to return to the Iron Horse Ranch and work it.

Duncan looked around the living room of the house his father had built for his mother. They'd outgrown the old homestead. His mother had argued that with four growing boys and one daughter, their family needed a larger home.

James McKinnon had immediately broken ground on the more modern cedar and stone home, with huge picture windows overlooking the Crazy Mountains his wife loved so very much. By the time Angus had turned ten, they'd moved in, each child having a room of his or her own.

He could live there. But was the house big enough for Fiona and Caity to live there full time?

Angus had moved out to his fiancée Bree's ranch to protect her and her mother. If he stayed there, he could be managing her ranch and need Duncan at the Iron Horse Ranch to run things there.

The sound of Caity's giggles made Duncan go in search of his little girl.

He found her in the kitchen with his mother and sister. Caity sat in a highchair as his mother fed her baby food from a jar.

The baby looked up at him and slapped the high-chair's tray in front of her.

Molly laughed. "She likes her green beans."

"Duncan loved green beans as well. He preferred them over carrots."

"I still hate stewed carrots," Duncan said, glancing around the large kitchen.

"If you're looking for Fiona, she's upstairs, getting a shower. Then she's going to sleep for a couple of hours." Molly grinned. "Mom and I are watching

Caity while Fiona sleeps." She leaned close and smiled in the baby's face.

Caity swung her chubby, green-bean-slathered fist at Molly.

Duncan's sister leaned back quickly. "Ha. You didn't get me that time."

Duncan's mother scooped another tiny spoonful of the green mush and popped it into Caity's mouth.

The baby pressed her lips together and hummed her approval. Green mush slid down her chin.

Molly used a towel to sop up the spillage. "Isn't she a complete doll?"

"She's not an inanimate toy," Duncan corrected. "She's a living, breathing human."

"Don't be such a grouch," Molly admonished. "Caity is just who we needed around here."

His mother nodded. "She's a breath of fresh air. So small and reliant on others to see to her needs."

Molly grinned at her mother. "And Mom needs to be needed."

Their mother nodded. "I do. It keeps me from ruminating about things I have no control over."

"We're going to find him," Duncan said, his lips tight, his fists clenching. They might find him, but finding him might not be the answer they were hoping for…if they found him dead.

Duncan's chest tightened.

When he and his brothers had arrived home, he'd had high hopes of finding his father alive. The more time that passed, the more he needed to come to grips that that might not happen.

With his mother and sister occupied and Caity surrounded by loving care, Duncan felt the need to get outside and do some manual labor. Working his muscles would help him burn off energy and keep him from getting stiffer.

He grabbed a biscuit from the counter and exited the house through the kitchen door. The morning sun had risen and shined down brightly on the day.

Duncan headed for the barn, working the soreness out of his bad leg as he walked.

The physical therapist had told him he would have discomfort in that leg for the rest of his life and a permanent limp. The damage to his muscle had been extensive. After the surgeon had worked on him, he'd laid it out, frank and holding no punches. Duncan would never have the same use of that leg. He'd be lucky to pass a fitness test running. Or limping. And if he couldn't pass a PT test, he couldn't perform his functions as an Army Ranger. He'd be more of a liability to the team than an asset.

One day, he was at the top of his game. The next, he was waiting for the inevitable decision the Medical Review Board would have to make. He'd be medically retired from the service. Benched from the game. Put out to pasture.

By the time he arrived at the barn, Duncan had worked out the stiffness, if not the pain.

Colin and Sebastian were inside saddling up a couple of horses.

The ranch foreman, Parker Bailey, led a bay gelding out of a stall and nodded silently toward Duncan.

Duncan looked around. "Where's Angus?"

"He headed over to Bree's ranch to mend fences that were damaged by a herd of mule deer which got tangled up in the barbed wire. He'll be gone until tomorrow."

"Bree and her mother need him over there more than we need him here," Colin said as he ran a curry comb over his gelding's flanks. "Especially since we're all home."

"Where are you heading?" Duncan asked.

"Out to the canyon where Dad disappeared," Sebastian said.

"We've been through there several times, already," Duncan said. "We didn't find anything."

Colin slung a saddle blanket over the gelding's back. "There's a lot of ground to cover in that canyon. We might have missed something small that could be just the clue to lead us to him and to Reed's killer."

Duncan nodded. He glanced toward their young foreman. "Are you going with them?"

He nodded. "I am, but I'll split off and check fences along the way. Had some cattle get out and wander onto federal land last week. I got them back, but I need to see if there are any other breaks that need patching."

"I'll only be a minute, saddling up," he said, heading for one of the stalls containing a gray mare he'd ridden on the few occasions he'd been home.

Colin held up a hand. "No need. You might want to stay here and keep an eye on your woman and child."

Duncan glanced toward the house. "You think whoever trashed Fiona's house will come to Iron Horse Ranch to threaten her here?"

"You don't know," Sebastian said. "If you go out searching for Dad with Angus over at Bree's place, that would leave Mom, Molly, Fiona and the baby by themselves."

Duncan frowned. "Molly is as good a shot as any one of us."

"Maybe so, but she doesn't have combat experience. She can hunt and target practice with the best of us, but she's never had to shoot a man. Will she?" Sebastian tilted his head and raised his eyebrows in challenge.

Duncan's mouth pressed in a firm line. "She's good, and she's very protective of family. She'd take care of the family."

"Are you willing to stake your life on that thought?" Colin asked. "Better yet, are you willing to stake Caity's life on that assumption?"

"You're forgetting that Fiona is a trained sheriff's deputy," Duncan said. "She can handle it."

He stopped with his hand on the latch securing the stall. The gray mare on the other side of the door pawed at the ground, eager to get out and run. He reached over and scratched the mare's ears. He sighed, knowing he couldn't leave the ladies, no matter how capable they were of defending themselves. "Sorry, old girl. Maybe later." Pushing away from the door, he helped Sebastian saddle his horse. "Find something, will ya?"

Sebastian looked across his horse's back, his lips twisting. "You know we'll try our best. We want him back as much as anyone."

Duncan nodded. "In the meantime, Parker, what needs doing around here?"

"Stalls always need to be mucked," Parker said.

"I was afraid you'd say that." Duncan saluted the foreman and his brothers as they rode out of the yard. Then he went to work cleaning out the stalls, stepping out of the barn several times to look up at the ranch house.

By the time he'd shoveled out the soiled straw and replaced it with fresh, his shoulders and leg throbbed. Several hours had passed, and no one had come out to check on him. He grinned. Likely his mother and sister were enjoying their time with baby Caity, and Fiona must still be asleep.

Duncan headed back to the house, anxious to see

his daughter. With Fiona asleep, he'd have time to shower and change into clean jeans and a T-shirt.

As he passed through the kitchen, he noted it was empty, and the highchair had been cleaned and set to rights. On his way to the staircase, he passed through the living room where his mother and Molly lay sprawled on couches, napping while Caity lay asleep in the playpen within easy reach.

After a quick glance at his daughter, Duncan climbed the stairs and caught himself short of barging into his old bedroom. He paused with his hand halfway to the door knob.

Fiona was sleeping in his bed.

He squelched the urge to go in anyway and see her sleeping, her red hair splayed out over the white pillowcase. He might have been inebriated when he'd made love to her fifteen months ago, but not so much so that he didn't remember how beautiful she'd been lying there naked in her bed, sleeping after their insane romp in the sack. Her skin had been silky soft, pale and creamy. The tomboy he'd grown up with had matured into a beautiful woman with curves that fit perfectly against his hard planes.

His groin tightened, and his cock pressed against the zipper on his jeans.

Now was not the time to relive that night. He smelled like the muck he'd cleaned out of the stalls, and he was drenched in sweat.

Dropping his arm to his side, he spun in the

direction of his mother's sewing room where she'd placed his clothes in a dresser next to the daybed.

With a clean shirt and jeans in hand, he back-tracked to the bathroom, showered the stench from his body and dressed.

When he left the bathroom, he didn't slow in front of his old bedroom, just walked past, carrying his boots down the stairs to the ground floor.

At the bottom, he sat on the steps and slipped his feet into the boots. Feeling more human and less like animal crap, Duncan crossed to the playpen, tiptoeing over the wooden floor to keep from waking the baby.

He stood in front of the playpen, staring down at his daughter. Her cheeks were a rosy pink and her lips a deep mauve. How could anyone so small be so perfect?

His heart swelled, and he fought the urge to lift her out of the pen and hold her close. He had six months of loving to catch up on. Unfortunately, it would have to wait until the child had slept at least for an hour.

Then, all bets were off. He wanted to get to know this child of his. How could Fiona have kept her from him for so long? He thought back over the past fifteen months. Much of that time had been spent deployed to the hills of Afghanistan. Had he known Fiona was pregnant, he would've been distracted. And he wouldn't have been able to get home much sooner. Many of his friends on his squad had had wives back in the States due to deliver any time. They'd paced and worried. One of his buddies had been evacuated back to his home station when his wife had gone into preeclamptic shock. She'd died giving birth to his baby boy. He'd left active duty and had taken a job as a janitor in an elementary school just to be able to raise his kid alone.

Duncan scraped his hand over his face. One little baby changed everything. His worry over his future in the military had flipped to concern that the Army might keep him on active duty.

Now, all he could think about was being there for Caity. He wanted to see her take her first steps, say her first word and ride her first horse. That was his little girl.

First and foremost, he had to protect her from whoever had threatened her mother. Caity looked healthy and happy. Duncan had no doubt Fiona was a good mother. Her choice of profession had him worried, though. Being a sheriff's deputy put her in harm's way. How had she managed to get this far as a single parent? Her hours had to be insane.

Caity needed two parents to make this work. Which led Duncan's thoughts back to Fiona.

He should marry her. That would give Caity the home she deserved and the parents she needed to see her through life.

Yeah. That's exactly what he needed to do. Marry Fiona.

His brow furrowed.

What if she didn't want to marry him?

His fists clenched. Damn it, she had to. He wanted to be just as much a part of Caity's life as she was.

Marriage was a commitment between two people who cared about each other. Duncan cared about Fiona. They'd been best friends for as long as he could remember. She had cared about him. Hadn't she seen him through several breakups with various girlfriends? Hadn't she stepped in when his prom date had suddenly backed out the day before prom? Wasn't she the one who'd rushed out onto the high school football field when he'd been knocked unconscious?

He'd loved Fiona like a best friend.

Then he'd gotten stupid drunk and made love to her.

The baby in the playpen was the result. He'd been certain he'd screwed up that perfect friendship forever. Hell, before they'd done the deed, Fiona had written letters to him. After…nothing. No word, no letters, no calls.

Duncan had missed those communications. He'd looked forward to getting her letters. They'd helped when he'd sat in a tent or foxhole far away from the home he loved. She'd filled him in on all the happenings in Eagle Rock, the crazy things the sheriff's department had to deal with on a daily basis from goats stuck in fences, to cattle roaming the highways and bears tipping over trashcans.

His last deployment had been all the harder without those letters. He'd been so homesick, he'd begun wondering if he really wanted to continue his career in the military. Then he'd been wounded, and the decision was being made for him.

So much was up in the air with his commitment to the military, his father's disappearance, the threat to Fiona and learning about the baby he hadn't known existed until that morning.

A hand touched his shoulder, making him jump. He spun to face the woman who'd turned his world upside down.

"Do you think your mother and sister would mind watching over Caity while I check on my house?"

"We'd gladly watch out for her," Molly answered. She sat up on the couch and stretched. "Unless Duncan wants a second shot at changing a baby diaper." Her face split in a wide grin. "I don't think I've seen my big, burly brother more out of his element. Wish I'd thought to record the moment. Caity would have loved seeing that when she was a little older."

Duncan glared at Molly. "I'd stay and figure it out, but if Fiona's heading back to her house, I'm going with her. However, I'm concerned over leaving the baby."

Molly brow furrowed. "We can take care of her. Mom's an expert at diaper changes."

"I'm not as worried about the diapers as I am about her safety. What if whoever threatened Fiona comes after Caity?"

Molly pushed her shoulders back. "I'm a better shot than you are. We can protect our little girl."

"You think someone will come after Caity?" Fiona asked. "I thought their beef was with me. Caity can't testify."

"No," Duncan said. "But they could use the baby as leverage to keep you from testifying."

Fiona's face blanched. "I don't know why I didn't think of that." She glanced out the window. "All I know is, I can't just stand by and let someone threaten me without finding out who it was and making them pay."

"We'll keep the doors locked and the windows buttoned up," Molly said. "I have my .40 caliber pistol and a loaded shotgun I can keep handy in case we come under attack."

Duncan's mother shook her head. "Let's hope it doesn't come to that."

"Hope might not be enough," Molly said, lifting her chin. "We'll be ready in case something happens."

"I'm not so sure it's a good idea to go looking for trouble," Duncan said. "The sheriff gave you a couple of days off. I'm sure he didn't intend for you to use it investigating the break-in."

"I can't sit back and do nothing." Fiona turned to Molly and his mother. "If you're all right watching Caity, I'm headed out to find the jerk who trashed my house." The fiery-haired Valkyrie headed for the door.

Duncan cursed beneath his breath.

"Duncan…" his mother warned.

"I know. I know," he grumbled. "I need to work on my words."

Molly tipped her head in the direction Fiona had gone. "You better catch her before she gets away."

Damned if his sister wasn't right.

CHAPTER 6

Fiona had her keys out and was reaching for the door handle on her SUV when Duncan caught up with her.

"We're going in my truck," he said, aiming for the truck parked next to her vehicle. As he walked, he tucked a handgun into the holster he'd slung over his shoulders and donned a leather jacket over all of it.

Fiona bristled. "You might be going in your truck, but I'm going in my SUV." She yanked open her door. Her rush of anger gave the motion more force than necessary, and the door bounced back into her arm. She winced and bit back a curse.

"Fine." Duncan rounded her SUV and folded his long limbs into the passenger seat. "I thought it might be better if we didn't show up in your vehicle. This vehicle might already be targeted." He shrugged. "But have it your way."

"I will." Rubbing her arm, she slid in behind the steering wheel. She hated when he made sense. But now that she'd committed to her SUV, she wasn't going to waffle. "You don't have to come with me, you know."

"Yes, I do," he said in a flat, matter-of-fact tone.

"I can handle myself without you along," she argued.

"Everyone needs backup when going into a sticky situation." He gave her a side-eyed look. "I'd say this one is as sticky as flypaper. Where do you plan to start?"

"My house then the sheriff's office. We'll decide from there."

Duncan nodded and secured his seatbelt. "Good plan."

They accomplished the drive into Eagle Rock without comment.

Fiona opened her mouth several times to say something but shut it before words came out. She wanted to know how he felt about having a baby dumped in his lap. How he felt about her keeping that information from him for so long. She wanted to know what the hell he was thinking about, sitting in the passenger seat, staring out the front windshield with his lips pressed in firm line.

Then again, she didn't want to know how angry he was, or how disappointed he was that he'd missed out on the first six months of his daughter's life.

Fiona felt terrible about taking so long to tell him. But she couldn't handle it if he insisted on marrying her for Caity alone. She wanted his love for herself as well as her child. Now, she'd never know if he could have loved her for just her.

She gripped the steering wheel and guided the vehicle down the highway toward Eagle Rock.

Perhaps it wouldn't be such a bad thing if he married her for the baby's sake. Wasn't it better to be with him than without him?

Fiona's chest tightened.

Though her life was in an uproar, she had to put it in perspective. At least, she had Caity. And Caity had a father.

Duncan's family situation was a whole lot more complicated than hers. With Mr. McKinnon missing, they couldn't move on. They were stuck in limbo until they found him, alive or dead.

Fiona prayed they'd find him alive. She wanted Caity to know her grandpa McKinnon. Having older parents, Fiona hadn't known her grandparents. They'd died before she was old enough to remember them.

James McKinnon was still young enough to be around for Caity to get to know and love him.

If he turned up alive.

The golden forty-eight hours, where families and lawmen held out hope to find the victim alive after an abduction, had long since passed. Fiona wasn't sure they'd find the McKinnon patriarch. If they did, most likely he'd be dead.

Fiona pulled into the driveway across from the cemetery and parked.

Duncan was out of the vehicle first and went ahead of Fiona up the steps to the front door.

Fiona joined him with the key. She had to step around him to insert the key into the lock—not that the lock was that effective with the doorframe now splintered. Still, she went through the motions.

Standing so close to him brought back memories of that night she'd helped him up to her room with the intention of letting him sleep off the consumption of too much booze.

He hadn't been a mean or sloppy drunk or she wouldn't have slept with him. Instead, he'd been nice and sexy.

She inhaled the scent that was one hundred percent Duncan and swallowed a sigh. Why did she have to be so in love with a man who didn't see her? Really see her. She'd been the invisible friend for so long that when he'd come on to her, she'd been so excited, she, the sober one, hadn't thought about protection.

Fiona pushed open the door.

Duncan touched her arm and moved past her into the house.

The cushions were still on the floor, the glass still strewn across the kitchen floor. Added to the mess was black latent print powder where techs from the police department had dusted for fingerprints.

Her home was a disaster. She couldn't bring Caity back to it until she'd thoroughly cleaned it and vacuumed up every sliver of glass. Caity would be crawling soon, and Fiona didn't want her to get any glass in her tiny hands and knees.

With Caity safely in the hands of the McKinnon women, Fiona had time to examine the damage. The intruder had gone in with the intent to destroy as much as possible. Perhaps, he'd hoped to scare her into moving out of Eagle Rock. He'd destroyed her second-hand couch and coffee table, broken her television, smashed nearly all of the dishes she'd had in her cabinets. If she hadn't come home when she had, he would have broken all of them.

"Things can be replaced," Duncan said.

She stared at him across the floor covered in broken dishes. He didn't understand that she didn't have much, and what she had was stuff she'd collected over the past year and a half from yard sales, thrift stores or hand-me-downs her friends had given her.

Fiona couldn't afford to buy all new items. Not on a deputy's salary.

She couldn't say any of that in front of Duncan. He'd feel sorry for her and offer to replace things at his expense. And that was the last thing she wanted. Duncan's pity. All her life, Fiona had prided herself on her independence and strength. She could ride a horse as fast and as long as any man, shoot straight and run fast. She didn't need a man to feel sorry for her. She needed to find who'd done this and make him pay. Scare tactics pissed her off.

The fact they'd hit her house and destroyed her baby's room not only made her mad, it made her more determined. She'd find the bastard and bring him down.

She saved her bedroom for last, knowing what she'd find on the wall and in no hurry to reread the harsh message.

Shut up or die.

"It has to be some of the Faulkner family's doings," Fiona said. "They're the only ones dumb enough to threaten local law enforcement and think they can get away with it."

Duncan nodded. "They were always getting in trouble in school. Everyone knew that if they wanted booze or drugs, they only had to find a Faulkner."

"They're still at it." Fiona's lips pressed together. "Only they've gotten craftier. They manage to elude us every step of the way. We suspect they've killed a number of drug runners over the past decade, but we haven't been able to pin it on them. They always manage to hide the evidence, or the witnesses disappear."

The writing on the wall stared back at her. The

red jumped out so much, it might as well have been a neon, blinking light.

"You all right?" Duncan asked, his tone warm and gentle.

Her eyes stung, but she refused to cry. Crying would accomplish nothing. "I'm fine." Fiona squared her shoulders and stepped out the back door and down the porch steps.

Tire tracks led away from the house into the woods.

"Want me to follow the tracks?" Duncan asked.

She'd thought of that as well but shook her head. "No use. There's a road on the other side of those woods. You'd lose the tracks at that point. I wish I'd seen the make and model of the motorcycle. Then I'd have something to go on. But I couldn't risk leaving Caity in the SUV that long. He might have circled around to the front of the house."

"You did the right thing," Duncan said. "Protecting Caity was more important."

She nodded and returned to the kitchen, using her boots to sift through the pieces of plates and glass, hoping to find something that could help her to identify the intruder. Nothing stood out. Until she cleaned up the debris, she wouldn't find anything of value in her investigation. She turned and headed for the front of the house.

"Are we leaving?" Duncan asked, falling in behind her.

"I am."

"I guess that means we're leaving." Duncan hurried around her and opened the driver's side door to her SUV.

Then he jogged around to the other side of the vehicle and climbed in.

She had already cranked the vehicle and shifted into reverse by the time he dropped into the passenger seat.

"Are you mad at me, or something?" he asked. "'cause from where I'm sitting, I'm the one with the main reason to be mad."

Fiona gripped the steering wheel, a jumble of thoughts roiling through her head. The relief of having told him about his daughter had quickly been replaced by other worries. Worries that included joint custody, visitation, child support and more. Before, she'd only had to worry about how to tell him. Now, they had decisions to make, and none of them would be easy.

Add to that, the problem at hand. Someone wanted her to keep her mouth shut. If it was over the Faulkner case, she'd be damned if she held back in a court case. The Faulkners had run roughshod over people in the county for long enough. It was time to shut them down.

Then again, was it worth risking her life or Caity's over a little conversation she'd overheard?

"I hope Sheriff Barron has some news for us,"

Fiona said, her jaw tight. "Too many threads are hanging loose for my liking."

"Too many are unraveling for my liking," Duncan said.

Moments later, they pulled up to the sheriff's building and got out.

"The sheriff isn't going to be happy about you showing up, demanding information about a case that has been reassigned to someone else," Duncan reminded her.

"He'll get over it. Our department is small. It's not like he has a lot of people he can hand it off to."

"Yeah, but you're going against his orders."

She gave him a sideways glance. "And when have you known me to stick to the rules?"

Duncan shook his head, his lips quirking upward at the corners. "I'd have thought working with the sheriff's department would've helped you learn to follow orders."

"I've got that down, for the most part."

"Glad to hear it." He opened the door for her and waited for her to pass through it before following her inside.

As she walked by, she inhaled his scent again and fought that urge to turn into him, wrap her arms around him and hold on tight.

He didn't belong to her. Just because she'd birthed his child didn't make him hers. As far as he was concerned, she was still the friend he'd had from high school. The friend he'd gotten pregnant on a drunken binge. People made mistakes. That didn't mean he should compound his mistakes by marrying a woman he didn't love any more than as a good friend.

Squashing her rampant thoughts, Fiona entered the sheriff's office. "What have you got on the fingerprints?"

Sheriff Barron looked up from his computer screen and cocked an eyebrow. "What part of *you're off the case* did you not understand?"

"It's my house. I think I have a right to know who was behind that ski mask."

"I'm working on them now. So far, all of the fingerprints processed belonged to you or Ruth. Did you notice whether or not your intruder was wearing gloves?"

Fiona closed her eyes and thought back to the image of the man standing in her hallway dressed all in black and wearing a black ski mask. She couldn't remember whether he wore anything on his hands because the moment he'd seen her, he'd let loose the butcher knives in his hands, aiming them at her.

Finally, she opened her eyes and shook her head. "No. I don't remember. Did you dust the butcher knives?"

The sheriff nodded and turned his attention back to the images on his screen. "I just started the comparison a few minutes ago. Should be getting something soon, if we get anything at all."

Fiona chewed on her lip. "Did you find the missing flashlight?"

The sheriff shook his head. "Hell, no. I spoke with Ellen. She said the only people who came in yesterday were the deputies at shift change."

Fiona frowned. "That would've been Cole Drennan and Jason Poindexter. They're solid. Could someone have slipped in while Ellen was handling a 911 call?"

"It's possible," the sheriff conceded. "But who could have gotten into the evidence locker without busting the lock?"

"Someone with a key," Duncan stated.

The sheriff sighed. "My thoughts exactly." He shook his head. "That would be me. I keep the key in this locked file drawer." He tapped the drawer by his knee. "The key to that drawer is on my key chain at all times."

"And I never see you without your keychain," Fiona's eyes narrowed. "Could someone have stolen the key from your house at night?"

The sheriff shook his head. "I have a rescue mutt with a big bark. Nothing gets past that dog without raising a ruckus. I would know if someone snuck into my house. Best alarm system ever."

Fiona studied the lock on the file drawer. It didn't appear to have been tampered with. She straightened. "Anything on James McKinnon's disappearance?"

"Not much," the sheriff said. "The blood samples

taken from the floor of the cave belonged to William Reed. Some of the blood wasn't Reed's or McKinnon's. We ran a search on the criminal database and failed to discover a DNA match. Whoever else bled that day hasn't made it to the database."

"Which means he hasn't been convicted of a crime that would get his DNA registered," Fiona finished. "Two of McKinnon's boys are back up in the canyon today, looking for more evidence."

"I hope they find something," the sheriff said. "Right now, we've run out of options."

"Is it possible one of your posse was in with Reed?" Fiona asked.

The sheriff shrugged. "When McKinnon went missing, we did a headcount of all the members of the posse we had. Everyone was there. Unless they had help out there in the canyon to take James away, I can't see how they could have shot Reed, hid James's b—" The sheriff shot a glance toward Duncan, cleared his throat and then continued, "and gotten back to the rest of the team."

Duncan's fists clenched. "Then they had to have had help, or there was someone else with Reed when my father found him. And that someone didn't want Reed or my father to identify him to anyone else."

Fiona bit down hard on her lip to keep from saying what that meant. If someone had been willing to kill Reed to keep him quiet, he'd be just as willing to kill James McKinnon for his silence.

Sheriff Barron looked down at the monitor on his desk. "Well, look what we have here." He leaned closer. "It appears we got a hit on the print from the butcher knives."

Fiona and Duncan crowded in behind the sheriff's chair and looked over his shoulder at the screen where two prints were displayed side by side.

"Whose is it?" Fiona asked, staring down that the bottom of the image, searching for a name.

"Wally Bing."

"Wally Bing?" Duncan echoed. "Is he still alive? I would have thought he'd have taken a long walk off a short cliff by now. As a teen, he didn't have the brains of a gnat."

"And yet, there are jobs for people like that," the sheriff said. "Barb employs those who are employable to do her dirty work."

"Know where he lives?" Fiona asked.

The sheriff narrowed his eyes. "If I did, I wouldn't tell you. I have a deputy on duty. I'll send him out to his place to question Wally and bring him in."

"Who's on duty?" Fiona asked.

"Cole has the day shift," Sheriff Barron said. "He can handle it."

"Not alone, he can't." Fiona looked across the sheriff's head to Duncan. "Are you going with him?"

"I am. Not that it's any of your business. You're not working today."

"If I go to Wally's place, it will be as a concerned

citizen, not as a representative of the sheriff's department."

"Seriously, Fiona, stay out of this," Duncan said. "You could make this situation even more complicated than it already is."

When Fiona clamped her lips shut to keep from telling the sheriff what her next moves would be, he sighed. "You're going to do whatever the hell you want, anyway, aren't you?"

Fiona still didn't say anything.

"Fine. But let me get in there first. Can't have you fouling up an investigation because you didn't collect the evidence legally."

The sheriff locked his computer, rose from his chair and stepped out into the hallway.

"Sheriff Barron," the 911 dispatcher ducked her head out the door, wearing her headset with the microphone shoved to one side. "We have a call from a woman about a bear in her yard. Her Yorkie is out there with it. She's afraid the bear will eat the Yorkie. Game warden is out on another call. Can you handle it?"

The sheriff grimaced. "I don't know. Do we have anymore bear spray?"

"Look in the storage closet behind the floor cleaner," she said and ducked her head back into her office.

The sheriff turned toward Fiona. "Leave Wally to me," he said with a stern look.

Fiona didn't respond.

With a sigh, the sheriff turned toward the storage closet. "I might as well be talking to a brick wall. Don't get yourself killed. I don't have time for the paperwork."

Fiona spun and headed for the exit.

"We're going to Wally's place, aren't we?" Duncan asked from behind her.

"Yup."

"Does he still live in the trailer park out by the old quarry?"

"Yup again," she said, pushing through the door. She didn't hold it for him, letting it close in his face.

CHAPTER 7

DUNCAN REACHED the SUV before Fiona, opened the door and stood in her way. "Perhaps I should drive."

She looked up at him with one eyebrow cocked. "Fine. I'd rather have both my hands free anyway, in case I have to fire my weapon."

Duncan frowned. "On second thought, you drive." He'd rather be the one to fire the shot if that became necessary. He wouldn't hesitate for a second if Fiona's life was on the line.

She shrugged. "Either way, I don't care. I just want to talk to Wally." She muttered something else he couldn't make out but sounded suspiciously like, "and beat the crap out of him for what he did."

His lips twitching, Duncan hurried around the SUV and dropped into the passenger seat. "Shouldn't you be in your uniform to arrest Wally?"

"I have a badge. He knows where I work. What more do I need?"

"A warrant or something?"

"We have the fingerprints on the butcher knives. That's my warrant." She shifted into reverse, backed out of her parking space in front of the sheriff's office and drove out onto Main Street.

A few minutes later, they were headed northwest on one of the smaller county roads toward the quarry where a company harvested gravel and base material for road projects.

A small community had been established three decades earlier of now dilapidated mobile homes that had seen better days.

Weeds grew around the cement blocks and dry-rotted tires holding up the trailers. Old cars rested on rusted jacks, their engines and wheels having been scavenged for parts.

With the sun dropping down below the ridgeline of the Crazy Mountains, dusk was settling in early, and the riffraff had gathered around a campfire ringed by gray mountain stones. Some smoked, others held cans or bottles of beer.

As Fiona pulled her SUV to a stop on the road, several of the men standing around straightened, their eyes narrowing.

Duncan hopped out of the car before Fiona had shifted into park. He bit down hard on the inside of his lip as he put all his weight on his bad leg. Pain shot up his thigh, but he fought to show no weakness in front of the rough looking group.

He focused on the men he knew from his school days. "Boyd, Johnny, Arlin." He nodded at each as he spoke his name. "Good to see you."

Boyd lifted his chin. "Duncan. What brings you out to these parts? I thought you'd be looking for your old man."

"I have been, but I'm looking for someone else right now."

All the gazes watching him narrowed and shifted as Fiona stepped out of the SUV.

Men who'd been sitting on tattered lawn chairs or tree stumps pushed to their feet.

One of the big guys, wearing a flannel shirt and dirty jeans stood, crossing his ham-hock-thick arms. "What is *she* doing here?"

Fiona didn't back down. "Boyd, how's community service going for you?" she asked, planting her fists on her hips.

Duncan almost laughed as the Valkyrie in Fiona came out in force.

The big guy snorted, and his eyes narrowed even more, but he didn't make another comment.

"We ain't done nothin' what warrants a visit from the deputy," Johnny said and threw his cigarette at Fiona's feet.

"How's your wife, Johnny?" Fiona stepped on the burning butt, dropping her arms to her side, her voice low and concerned. "Has she been using her nebulizer for her asthma?"

Johnny hesitated before he nodded and shot a glance toward the other men standing around. "She ain't had another attack since I quit smokin' in the house, like you said."

"Glad to hear it. She was in a bad way the other night when we took her to the clinic."

"Yes, ma'am." He looked at the ground, refusing to meet the gazes of the other men.

"What do you want, Deputy?" Arlin said.

"Someone trashed my house around six thirty this morning. I'm willing to forgive and forget, but I want to know why and whether I can expect it to happen again."

Duncan studied the men as they looked at each other accusingly. It was clear they hadn't heard about the break-in. They weren't the ones responsible.

"It weren't me, Deputy," Johnny said.

"Did you do it?" Boyd asked Arlin.

Arlin spit on the ground at Boyd's feet. "Hell, no. I don't pick on girls, like some of you do."

Boyd's fists clenched. "I sure as hell didn't."

Another man Duncan recognized as Skeeter Jones shook his head. "You're barkin' up the wrong tree. None of us done it."

"I didn't say any of you did it. But one of the residents of this fine community did." Fiona lifted her chin, her tone hardening. "And we have a match on the fingerprints from the knife he threw at me."

"Who was it," Johnny asked. "We'll take care of him."

Arlin stepped toward Johnny. "You ain't gonna take care of nothin'. We don't turn on our own here."

"If someone's trying to kill the deputy, who's to say he won't try to slit our throats if given half a chance?" Johnny reasoned. "You gonna trust someone like that to sleep in the trailer next to yours?"

"Shut up, Johnny," Boyd said. "Or someone will slit your throat for talking too much." He turned to Fiona. "Who did you say it was that tried to kill you?"

"I'm looking for Wally Bing," Fiona said. "I understand he lives in one of the trailers."

"He does, but he's not here," Arlin said. "Guess you'll have to come back when he is."

"Do you mind showing us which trailer it is he lives in?" Duncan asked.

Boyd shrugged. "Last one on the left. Watch out on the steps. Some of them have rotted through." He sank down on the stump he'd been sitting on before they'd arrived and tossed back a swig of beer.

Duncan cupped Fiona's elbow. "Come on."

She pulled her arm free and faced the men. "Thank you," she said, her tone even, her face gentle as if she understood how men could become so desperate. Then she turned and walked beside

Duncan to the trailer at the end with the rotting steps.

Careful not to put too much weight on the broken slats, Duncan climbed the steps and knocked on the door of the single-wide, forty-foot trailer that had probably been assembled in the 1970s. The aluminum siding had long since faded to a dull gray and was peeling upward where it had been dented. The door had a yellowed window with a tattered curtain covering it.

Duncan knocked on the door and waited to the side. If the man was inside and decided to start a shooting war against the person knocking, Duncan didn't want to be on the receiving end of the bullets.

No one answered.

Duncan gripped the door handle.

"What are you doing?" Fiona whispered.

"Going to see if he's inside." Duncan twisted the knob and pulled on the door.

It didn't open.

Fiona let go of a rush of air. "It's locked. He's not home. Let's go." She started to turn.

Duncan twisted and gave it a hard jerk.

The door opened and a stench like nothing Fiona had ever smelled before wafted out. She stepped backward and covered her mouth. "Holy crap. What is that smell?"

Duncan reached inside and flipped on the light switch. No lights came on. "Looks like he didn't pay his electric bill." He dug in his pocket for his keychain and held it up to the darkness On the end of the keychain he had a miniature flashlight. He pushed the button, and the room lit up enough so they could see inside.

The place was a mess with dirty clothes lying on the rotted floor and Styrofoam food boxes left lying on surfaces piled with trash.

Duncan pulled his T-shirt over his nose and stepped inside. "Wally, if you're in here, you might as well come out," he called out.

"Duncan, he's not here. Let's go."

"I'll be right out," he said and stepped over a pair of worn out boots and a dumbbell lying in the middle of the floor. At the back of the trailer was a bedroom completely filled with an old bed and a nasty, stained mattress. And it was empty other than a tattered, dirty blanket lying in a heap.

Fiona had said the man who'd trashed her place had worn all black and a black ski mask. Duncan didn't see any signs of either in the trash piled on every surface. He backed out of the trailer, stepped onto the porch and closed the door behind him firmly, before he dropped the front of his shirt and sucked in a deep breath of fresh air.

Fiona waved for him, shooting nervous glances around. "Get down here."

Duncan ignored the stairs and jumped off the

porch to the ground beside Fiona, landing with a grimace, his bad leg giving slightly.

She grabbed his arm and led him away from the trailer. "Did you see anything?"

"So, you'll break the rules with your boss but not with the law?"

"Of course. I'm in law enforcement. I can't go around breaking the law," she said in a harsh whisper.

Duncan grinned. "You can't, but I can."

"And if I were being a good deputy, I'd arrest you right now."

"So, you'll break the law for the right person?" He grinned and waved toward the men still sitting around the fire. "Good to see you guys. If you see Wally, tell him we're looking for him."

Darkness had settled over the valley, with only the faint glow of receding sunshine still shining over the ridges of the Crazy Mountains.

Duncan held the door for Fiona to climb in behind the wheel. Then he rounded the car and got in on the other side. "Drive, sweetheart. I'm not sure how much longer those gentlemen will behave themselves."

Fiona shifted into gear and drove away from the trailer community and back out onto highway.

"Where to now?" he asked, glad that encounter was over.

"The Faulkners' place," Fiona said.

"No." Duncan shook his head. "Not at night. You need broad daylight to confront that lot."

"I need to find Wally. I need to know who put him up to what he did."

"You have to know it was the Faulkners."

"I know," she said, her shoulders slumping. "And I know you're right. Confronting them on their turf at night isn't a good idea."

Duncan reached over and touched her arm. "Then, babe, don't do it."

She drew in a long, deep breath and let it out slowly as she pulled onto the highway leading into Eagle Rock. "Okay. It'll wait until tomorrow. We'll find Wally and get the truth out of him. Right now, I want to get back to the ranch before Caity goes down for the night. I need my snuggle time with my baby."

Duncan's heart swelled at the sound of longing in Fiona's voice. She loved their baby.

He already loved Caity, and he hadn't known her long.

Fiona increased their speed, sending the old SUV down the road in a hurry to get back to Iron Horse Ranch and Caity.

They rounded a corner in the road and nearly hit something lying in the road.

At the last minute, Fiona swerved to avoid the large lump and ran off the pavement onto the shoulder. She brought the vehicle to a halt and took her hands from the wheel.

In the light from the dash, Duncan could see that her hands were shaking.

"What was that?" he asked, turning in his seat to look back.

"I don't know, but I have a bad feeling." She gripped the steering wheel and made a U-turn in the road, careful to watch for headlights of any oncoming vehicles. When her SUV faced the opposite direction with its headlights shining on the lump in the road, she gasped.

Duncan's stomach lurched. He threw open the door, jumped out and ran toward the object.

Lying in the middle of the road was the body of a man who'd apparently been run over.

Duncan moved the man enough to press his fingers to the base of his throat.

He tried several times but couldn't find a pulse.

Fiona knelt beside him. "Is he?"

He nodded. "Dead."

Fiona held a radio in her hand. She pressed the button on the side and spoke into the mic. "Ellen, send the coroner." She gave their location. "And notify Sheriff Barron...we found Wally Bing. He's dead."

So much for getting home to hug their baby.

Over an hour later, they were still sorting through the crime scene. Fiona had set out flares on either end of the curve in the road to slow traffic. She directed cars and trucks around the body until the sheriff and the ambulance arrived. After they'd taken pictures of the scene, Wally's body was loaded into the ambulance and taken to the coroner's office in Bozeman.

By that time, it was getting late.

Fiona and Duncan had filled in the sheriff on their visit to the trailer park near the quarry.

"You two might as well go home," the sheriff said. "Nothing more we can do here tonight."

"What about talking to the Faulkners?" Fiona asked.

Duncan shook his head, but he didn't have to.

Sheriff Barron said, "It'll wait until morning. Anyone visiting them at night has a death wish."

"But if they did this, they need to be brought to justice," Fiona argued. "Sooner than later."

"I agree. But I plan to live to see my next birthday, which, by the way, is two weeks from today, and I like pie versus cake. But what I mean is, they know the hills better than anyone, and they would have the advantage, especially in the dark."

Fiona nodded. "I know you're right. Duncan said the same thing. I'm just fed up with them getting away with murder. We have to find that flashlight. Mark Faulkner should be in jail for life."

"Hopefully the coroner can provide evidence we can use to nail the bastard."

"What are the chances of nailing them for a hit and run?" Fiona's mouth twisted. "It was probably dark out here when it happened. There were no eyewitnesses."

"There's the possibility of finding DNA evidence on whatever vehicle hit him," the sheriff said.

Fiona snorted. "If we find it before they wash away the evidence, which they seem to excel at. Which means, getting to them tonight."

"We're not going tonight," the sheriff said, his tone firm, his face set in stone.

"Fine. First thing tomorrow morning, then." Fiona drew in a breath and let it out.

Duncan cupped her elbow. "Can we go home now? I just learned today that I have a baby girl. I'd like to see her."

Fiona gave him a weak smile. "We're going home." She let him lead her to the SUV and even let him take the driver's seat.

Duncan liked the way *home* sounded on Fiona's lips. He liked that he was going home with her to see their daughter. More than that, he wished it was permanent. How would he convince his friend of so many years that he wanted to be more than friends?

He wasn't sure where to start, but he had to do it. For Caity. For Fiona. For himself.

CHAPTER 8

MENTALLY AND PHYSICALLY DRAINED, Fiona dragged her feet up the steps into the house. Duncan's warm hand on her arm gave her strength, and the thought of seeing Caity made her push forward when she wanted to drop to the floor and go to sleep there.

As a sheriff's deputy, she'd been exposed to many different situations, from loose livestock to murder victims. The dead bodies always took their toll on her emotionally, which took its toll on her physically.

Having Duncan by her side through it had been a godsend. She'd never tell him that. She was a trained deputy. Everything that had happened that night had been what she was expected to handle whenever and wherever it occurred. Normally, she did and went home to Caity, tired but determined to power through for the sake of her small family.

Perhaps having Duncan there made her weak,

made her lean on him more than she should. Or was it the emotional turmoil of loving him and knowing he didn't love her in return that was draining her energy?

She suspected it was a combination of everything.

Duncan's mother met them in the living room, a frown furrowing her brow. "You two must be exhausted. Caity's upstairs with Molly, who's getting her bath before she goes to bed. You have time to eat before she's out of the tub. Come straight to the kitchen. I have a roast warming in the oven."

Fiona's stomach rumbled despite the fact she'd been with a dead body recently. She realized she hadn't had anything to eat that day.

Hell, had it only been a day?

She felt is if she'd lived through a week in that one day. From the break-in, to the big reveal to Duncan, to confronting a trailer park full of belligerent men and, finally, a dead suspect in the road, it had been a very eventful day.

Add the fact she'd gotten less than four hours of sleep. No wonder she was tired.

She followed Mrs. McKinnon to the kitchen, with Duncan trailing behind her.

Voices carried down the hallway before they arrived at the large, farm kitchen.

Duncan's brothers, Colin and Sebastian, were seated at the table, polishing off the last of their meals.

"About time you came home," Colin said. "We were about to dig into your portions of that roast." He held out a hand to Sebastian. "Pay up."

Sebastian pulled his wallet from his pocket and handed Colin a twenty. "I had you pegged for making a stop at the Blue Moose Tavern for dinner and a beer, before making the trek home. Colin won that bet."

Mrs. McKinnon pulled a pan filled with a juicy roast out of the oven and set it on top of the stove.

The smells in the kitchen made Fiona's knees weak.

"Sit," Duncan said, and guided her into a chair at the table. "What do you want to drink?"

She looked up at Duncan, wanting to fall into his arms and stay there the rest of the night. "Would it be too much to ask for that beer 'Bastian was talking about?"

"There's some in the fridge," his mother said.

Duncan grabbed two longneck bottles from the refrigerator, twisted off the tops and handed her one.

Fiona tipped the bottle up and drank half the bottle before she turned it up and set it on the table.

"Rough day?" Sebastian asked.

"Pretty much," she answered.

"Tell us about it," Colin urged.

Fiona turned to Duncan. "You want to fill them in? I don't have it in me."

He nodded and gave his brothers and mother the digest version of their trying day.

Colin whistled. "Wally Bing's dead?"

Sebastian shook his head. "I'm surprised he lasted as long as he did. He wasn't the sharpest tool in the shed."

"Any idea who ran him over?" Sebastian asked. "Wait, let me guess…one of the Faulkners?"

"We don't know," Duncan said. "The sheriff didn't want to venture out to their place at night."

"Wise move. They know those hills better than anyone," Colin said.

Sebastian nodded. "And they're skilled with long-distance marksmanship. Could have used them as snipers in Iraq and Afghanistan."

"If you could trust them not to shoot you in the back," Duncan added.

"Did they determine cause of death? Was it being hit by a vehicle? Or were there any gunshot wounds?"

"Didn't see any holes in his body," Duncan said. "But we did see tread marks across his clothing and skin."

"Death by vehicular manslaughter." Colin shook his head. "Wally probably got what he deserved. Now, if only the Faulkners could be served up their just desserts."

"We've been trying to nail them for years, but they're perfecting the art of dodging the law and hiding the evidence." Fiona took another draw on the beer. Finally, she could feel the tug of a buzz pulling her away from the strain and stress of the day. She relaxed her shoulders and rolled her head around, loosening the muscles in her neck.

Duncan set his beer on the table beside hers. "Let me." He placed a cool hand and a warm hand on the back of her neck and gently dug into her tight muscles.

Before long, his cold hand warmed as he worked out the knots and strain.

Fiona let her chin drop to her chest and moaned.

"When you're done there, I could use a massage," Colin suggested.

"Bite me," Duncan quipped.

Colin snorted. "Oh, I get it, you'll massage the pretty girl, but when it comes to a brother, you draw the line?"

"Got that right," Duncan said, his hands working magic.

Not only was he working out the pain and stress, he was waking her up to other possibilities she wasn't ready to explore.

Fiona lifted her head and sat up straight. "Thanks. I think I'll live, now."

Duncan swallowed some of his beer and crossed the room to help his mother.

Fiona's gaze followed him, noting the way he

limped slightly. She'd been so busy worrying about the break-in she hadn't asked him about his injury.

She remembered when it had happened. Sheriff Barron had been on the phone with the Red Cross. They wanted him to notify the family of a local soldier that he'd been injured in a helicopter crash.

Fiona had been in the office filling out a report when the news came through. Her breath had lodged in her throat, and her heart stopped beating as she'd waited for the name of the injured soldier.

When Duncan McKinnon's name had been mentioned, Fiona had felt as if she'd been sucker punched in the gut. Bile rose up from her belly. She had to swallow several times before she could ask if Duncan was all right.

The sheriff had nodded. Duncan had been airlifted out of theater to Landstuhl, Germany, where he'd been taken into surgery. The injury hadn't been life-threatening, but he'd be shipped back to the States soon after for rehab.

The sheriff had gone out to the Iron Horse Ranch to notify Duncan's parents.

When he'd returned, the sheriff had smiled, saying the family had already been on a video call with Duncan, and he'd assured them that he was okay and there was no need for them to fly out to Germany. He'd said he'd be up and running before long.

Fiona had breathed a sigh of relief and, at the

same time, she'd wondered how truthful he'd been in his conversation with his folks.

Duncan had a habit of downplaying injuries. Since his father had been in special forces, he'd raised his children to be tough. When they fell, he told them to get up, brush themselves off and keep going. He'd expected no less of them than he'd expected of himself.

Had Fiona been able, she would have flown out to see him when he'd arrived at the military hospital in Bethesda, Maryland. But she'd had a small baby to care for and no extra money to afford the plane ticket to get there. Instead, she'd had to be content getting second-hand news from the Eagle Rock grapevine concerning Duncan's recovery process.

She'd stopped writing letters to him after their night together because she hadn't been able to think of anything to say when all she'd wanted to write was, *I love you with all my heart.*

She'd figured it would be better for him and her that he not be burdened with her soppy love while he was trying to focus on staying alive. After she'd discovered she was pregnant, she never could come up with the words to tell him. An announcement like that needed to be delivered in person.

Duncan turned toward her with two plates of food and walked back to the table.

He didn't limp as much this time.

Fiona could tell by the strain in his face that he was working hard not to limp in front of her.

"At least you figured out who trashed your place," Sebastian said. "As for us, we spent several hours combing the canyon, searching caves and trails."

Duncan settled in the seat beside Fiona. "And?"

Sebastian dropped his hand to the table with a resounding thud. "Nothing."

"Not a damn thing," Colin agreed.

Mrs. McKinnon sighed and blinked back the moisture in her eyes. "I know he's out there. I just know it." She brought two glasses filled with orange juice to the table. "Anyone want coffee?"

"I do," Duncan said. "But I can get it myself."

His mother held up her hand. "Please, let me get it for you."

"Mom, you work too hard. You should be the one sitting down."

"No, really. I don't need to sit," she said and hurried toward the coffee maker.

Sebastian reached across the table and grabbed Duncan's wrist, keeping him from getting up from the table.

Duncan glared down at the hand, and then caught Sebastian's gaze.

His brother gave a slicing motion across his neck and whispered. "Let her do for you. She needs to stay busy."

Fiona smiled at the concerned frown Duncan

shot toward his mother's back. Then he sank back in his seat. "In that case, thanks, Mom."

She poured a cup of steaming brew and brought it to him.

He took it and thanked her.

Fiona reached beneath the table and laid a hand on his knee. The man loved his family. His father's disappearance had to be killing him. But seeing his mother's distress only added to the heartache.

His hand slipped over hers and remained, warm and comforting.

She knew how Mrs. McKinnon felt. Fiona had lost the man she loved fifteen months ago when he'd returned to active duty. Staying busy had been the only thing she could do to maintain her sanity and not let depression get her down too low.

During her pregnancy, she'd had her emotional highs and lows that went along with the hormonal changes. Carrying a baby while working as a sheriff's deputy had had its own challenges, the least of which was being taken seriously. But she'd refused to quit. She'd had to work to save money for her recuperation after delivery.

Fiona dug into her meal, knowing she had to keep up her strength. Caity needed her, and she had a job to do. Even if she wasn't working officially as a deputy for the next couple of days, she sure as hell was going to get to the bottom of the attack on her house and the murder of Wally Bing.

She didn't think for a minute that Wally Bing had any reason to trash her house and threaten her to keep her mouth shut. That message on the wall had Mark Faulkner or his family written all over it.

Fiona hoped like hell the sheriff kept Faulkner in jail a little longer. One less Faulkner to deal with brought her a little closer to evening out the playing field.

It was only a matter of time before the district attorney caught wind of the fact the flashlight had gone missing. Then he'd demand Faulkner be released based on the lack of evidence.

When she was finished with her dinner, Fiona carried her plate to the sink.

Duncan followed.

"Don't worry about the dishes," Mrs. McKinnon said. "I'll take care of them. You two need to get upstairs before Caity goes to sleep."

"Thanks, Mrs. McKinnon," Fiona said.

"Call me Hannah," she said. "Mrs. McKinnon was all right when you were a child, but now it makes me feel old." She smiled. "Or call me Mom. You spent enough time out here growing up, you might as well be one of my own." She hugged Fiona. "And thank you for giving me the best gift anyone could ever want." She sniffed and wiped a tear from her cheek. "My first grandbaby." She laughed. "Look at me getting all emotional."

Fiona's eyes welled. "I'm sorry I didn't tell you all sooner."

"What's past is past. We have a whole lifetime of love ahead of us with Caity." She hugged her again. "Now, go before I turn into a weepy mess."

Fiona stepped aside.

Duncan hugged his mother. "I love you, Mom. We'll do all we can to make things right."

She nodded. "Thank you, son. I know you all will do your best. I'll be up later to kiss Caity goodnight."

Fiona led the way up to Duncan's old bedroom and eased open the door.

Someone had moved a rocking chair into the room, and Molly was sitting in it, rocking and singing softly to Caity.

The baby's eyelids drooped, but then she'd jerk back awake and stare around the room as if she were fighting sleep.

"We've been rocking since we finished our bath," Molly said softly.

"She fights it all the way to lights out," Fiona informed her. "Want me to take over?"

Caity looked up, spied Fiona and grinned. She held out her arms and bounced in Molly's lap.

Molly laughed. "Traitor. I see where Aunt Molly ranks in the scheme of things."

Fiona chuckled and took Caity into her arms. "Hey, Moon Pie. You're giving Aunt Molly a complex."

Molly got up from the chair. "Want to sit here?"

"No thanks," Fiona said. "I usually lie on the bed and let her wiggle and kick until she gets it out of her system. When she falls asleep, I move her to her crib."

"Now, you tell me." Molly nodded. "I'll remember next time I have the pleasure of keeping her. When might that be?" Molly asked eagerly.

"I don't want to wear out my welcome. Ruth Henson usually keeps Caity when I work, day or night. I can get her to watch Caity, if I need to."

"Ruth's a lovely person, but you can't leave Caity in town without protection," Molly said. "Not until we get to the bottom of the threat to your life." Molly shook her head. "No, she needs to stay with us until we can be certain she's safe. Mom and I can trade off watching her."

"We can have one of us men stay around the house and barn at all times in case someone tries something stupid," Duncan said, holding up a hand. "I know you can handle anything, but if you're caring for Caity, you might not be aware of what's going on outside the walls of the house."

Molly nodded. "Good point. The more eyes the better."

"Are you available to watch Caity tomorrow while I go out and question people about the break-in?" Fiona asked. She shot a quelling glare at Duncan. "And don't try to talk me out of it. I have to do this. Caity and I won't be safe until we resolve the issue."

"What happened today?" Molly asked. "Did you find the man who trashed your place?"

"We did," Fiona said and gave Molly a brief rundown of what had occurred.

When she'd finished, Molly let out a low whistle. "Wow. And people wonder how the Crazy Mountains got that name. There be crazy folk up there in those hills." She winked, and then sobered. "But seriously, you're going up to the Faulkners' place? Please tell me Duncan's going with you, armed to the teeth?"

Duncan nodded. "I'll be there. There's no way in hell she's going up there alone."

"Yeah. They'd kill her and hide the body before anyone knew she'd gone missing." Molly sighed. "I've thought a number of times about the Faulkners, that they might have had a hand in Dad's disappearance. While you're up there, ask them where they were when someone shot William Reed."

Duncan nodded. "I will."

"As for watching Caity tomorrow," Molly grinned. "Mom and I would gladly spend more time getting to know her. She's such a happy baby."

As if she knew Molly was talking about her, Caity batted a fist at her and giggled.

Molly caught the little fist and kissed her fingers. "Sleep tight, little one. Your mommy and daddy are so lucky to have you." Molly left the room, closing the door behind her.

"Come on, sweetie, time for you to go to sleep. It's

past your bedtime." Fiona laid Caity in the middle of the bed and laid down beside her.

"Mind if I join you?" Duncan asked.

Her heart leaped. "Not at all. Now that she's learned how to roll over on her own, I have to keep a close eye on her, or she'll roll right off the bed. I had the bed in my room pushed up against the wall to keep that from happening."

"I thought it was just because the room was so small."

Fiona shrugged. "That too, but mostly so I could keep Caity from falling off the bed."

Duncan sank down on the other side of the bad and hemmed her in with his long body.

For a few joyous minutes Fiona basked in the feeling of family. Caity's family. Mommy, daddy and baby. Her heart swelled, and she felt more optimistic about the future than she had for a long time.

Then she crashed to the earth with the knowledge it was all a fantasy. Duncan was there for Caity, not her. She had no hold on Duncan, and he didn't want one on her.

Her eyes stung.

Damn. She couldn't cry.

Duncan sat up. "Look, I know I could use a shower before getting too close to Caity. Do you think she'll go to sleep before I get back?"

Caity kicked and giggled, reaching for Duncan's shirt with her chubby little fist.

"I doubt it. She's pretty wound up right now."

"I'll be back before you notice I'm gone." He disappeared from the room, leaving Fiona to get a grip on her emotions.

Why did she have to be such a mess around Duncan? She wasn't pregnant. Her hormones had leveled out since giving birth to Caity. She had no excuse for being so out of control.

Her eyes welled again, and a single tear slid down her cheek and fell onto the comforter.

The man had a way of turning her inside out, without even trying. How was she going to get through the next few days or weeks with him around? When was he going back to active duty?

The thought of Duncan leaving again made another tear slip from the corner of her eye and land on the comforter.

Caity rolled her direction and batted her hand at her face.

"Yeah, your mommy is in love with a man who sees her as one of the guys. A buddy. A best friend. Sucks to be in the 'friend zone.'" She laughed, the sound catching on a sob. "I'd better get over it quickly, because it does no good to cry."

Caity, sensing her mother's sadness, puckered up and cried.

"Hey, hey. I'm okay." She smiled down at Caity, though her heart was breaking. "You're okay." Then she felt the baby's diaper. "Well, maybe a dry diaper and some milk will make you smile."

If only a diaper and milk worked for broken hearts as well. She chuckled at the image in her mind, lifted Caity into her arms and carried her down to the kitchen where she warmed a bottle of formula. With the baby reaching greedily for the bottle, Fiona hurried back up the stairs before Duncan turned off the water.

She sat in the bed and held Caity in her arms, letting the baby hold the bottle herself…with a little help balancing it, since it was so full.

Caity sucked down half the bottle by the time Duncan returned to sit on the other side of the bed.

His hair was still wet, like he'd rushed out of the bathroom, afraid he'd miss something

"You want to feed her while I shower?" Fiona asked.

"Sure." His brow furrowed. "What do I do?"

Fiona laughed. "You hold her. She'll do the rest. If she finishes before I get back, lean her up or lay her across your shoulder and pat her back to get her to burp. Bubbles in her belly hurt."

"That simple?" he asked, not looking all that confident. He held out his arms.

Fiona settled Caity in her father's arms.

Caity's gaze switched from Fiona to Duncan and back. Her pretty little brow wrinkled, and she reached with one hand toward Fiona.

"It's okay. Daddy will take care of you while I get cleaned up. I'll be right back." She stepped away, out of Caity's view and gave Duncan a thumbs-up signal. Then she grabbed panties, a sleep shirt and ran for the bathroom.

Once inside, she stared at her reflection in the mirror, wondering who the woman was staring back at her. She'd worked hard all her life to be a confident, capable human. In a matter of seconds, one man made her feel like a bowl of soupy pudding. Pudding she'd like to smear all over his body and lick off one delicious swipe at a time.

Fiona moaned.

She turned on the water, stripped out of her clothes and stepped under the spray, letting it glide over her skin, washing away the smell of Wally's trailer and death.

If she and Duncan were truly a couple, she'd have Molly watch Caity while they both showered together.

To save water.

Fiona snorted. Ha. They'd waste more by making love against the cool tiles, and then spend the rest of the hot water exploring every inch of each other's bodies, with a little soap and a lot of touching.

She moaned again and brushed her breasts with the tips of her fingers. Fiona wished the fingers were Duncan's. He'd tweak her nipples until they hardened into tight little beads. Then he'd slide his hands over her ribs and down the triangle of hair covering her sex.

Her fingers traced the path she imagined Duncan would take and parted her folds, flicking the strip of flesh between.

A shock of sensations ripped through her, making her knees weak and her body tremble.

How much better would it feel if the hands were coarse and larger, scraping across her tenderness.

She flicked herself again and leaned back, letting the warm water rush down her chest and belly to that special place.

Why was she torturing herself? Wouldn't it be easier to ask Duncan to make love to her? They didn't have to commit to anything. Just have sex and call it a day.

Maybe, being sober now, he'd think it was a little too weird making love to the person who'd been his best friend for so long.

The water turned cooler, reminding her she wanted to get back to tuck Caity into her bed.

Ignoring the ache deep in her belly, Fiona rinsed the shampoo from her hair and the soap from her body. Then she turned off the water and rubbed her skin dry with a big fluffy towel.

After dressing in panties and a long sleep shirt that covered her from neck to knees, she tossed her clothes into the dirty clothes basket and ran her brush through her wet hair. She studied herself in the mirror again and didn't like what she saw. With her hair wet and slicked back from her face and wearing a shirt that did nothing for her figure, she appeared to be androgynous. She could easily pass for a boy.

She searched beneath the sink and found a blow dryer. Within minutes, she had her hair half-dried and curling around her shoulders.

The last time she'd been with Duncan, he'd been drunk and had complimented her on her hair. She'd worn it down that night at the Blue Moose Tavern.

Why she cared how she looked, she didn't know. It wasn't like Duncan was interested. He was only interested in her as the mother of his baby.

With a sigh, Fiona opened the bathroom door and crossed the hall to the bedroom she'd be sharing with Caity. Though she was wearing her night clothes, they weren't revealing, and she'd worn less swimming in the creek with Duncan and his brothers.

Still, she felt the cool night air creep up her legs, reminding her she was almost naked beneath the night shirt.

As she opened the door, her heart did a somersault.

Caity lay in the middle of the bed with a pillow on one side and Duncan on the other.

Both were sound asleep.

Fiona stood for a long moment drinking her fill of the sight. The two people she loved most were beautiful in their sleep. She committed the image to memory before she bent, lifted Caity in her arms and carried her to her crib.

She pressed her lips to her baby's soft cheek and laid her in her bed, tucking a soft blanket around her. "Sleep tight, sweet Caity," she whispered.

When she turned back to the bed, Duncan hadn't moved. His chest rose and fell in an even and deep rhythm.

Fiona hated to wake him and send him down the hallway to the bedroom where his mother had moved his things. If it weren't for Caity, Fiona would have slept in the other room.

She looked at the wooden rocking chair and shook her head. It was great for rocking a baby to sleep, but not for an adult to spend the night in.

Her gaze returned to the bed with Duncan taking up only half of the space. If she was very careful, Fiona could slip in beside him. If she woke before him, she could slip out as quietly, and he'd never know the difference.

But she would.

Pushing that thought to the back of her mind, she slipped beneath the comforter and turned her back to the man. If she didn't see him, she wouldn't be tempted to touch him.

Fiona told herself she was there to sleep. Nothing else. And, by golly, she was going to sleep.

Ha. Right. Easier said than done when the man

she loved was close enough she could roll over and be in his arms.

Closing her eyes, she willed her body to stop humming, her core to stop aching and her mind to let go of the fantasy.

Sometime, much later, she finally fell asleep.

CHAPTER 9

DUNCAN STIRRED IN HIS BED, bumping into something warm and solid beside him. The form was soft and not unpleasant, so he moved closer and threw his arm around it. He couldn't remember having a heated pillow, nor did pillows move.

And this one did, rolling over into the crook of his arm. Something tickled his nose, bringing him to the brink of being awake.

He blinked his eyes open and stared down at red hair in the soft glow of a nightlight that had been placed in one of the electrical outlets.

As he came fully awake, he realized where he was and who was lying in his arms, stirring him even more awake in much more dangerous ways.

Her rich red hair splayed out across the white pillowcase, much as it had the night he'd made love to her. The woman he'd always considered a friend had changed. She'd gone from a gangly, athletic teen to a shapely female with a body that had awakened in him a desire he'd never felt for any other woman.

Yes, he'd had too much to drink that night, but he hadn't been so drunk he hadn't known what he was doing.

Okay, well, he had skipped the part about using protection. But they'd been hot and heavy into making love before it had occurred to him. By then, it had been too late. He'd come inside her, and there was no going back after that.

Now, she lay in his arms, her cheek resting against his chest, her arm draped over his hip.

If he moved just a little, her hand would drop lower.

And just like that, his cock stiffened.

Like that night fifteen months ago, when he'd wanted her so badly, he'd lost his mind and taken what she'd so willingly given without thoughts of consequences. And he'd had to leave the next day.

Going from friends to lovers was not what he'd had in mind when he'd gone home on leave. But things happened when alcohol and a beautiful woman were involved. He remembered seeing her for the first time after his long absence.

He wouldn't have recognized her if not for that bright, auburn hair hanging in riotous curls down her back.

God, she'd been beautiful. And he'd wanted her.

Not like a best friend wants a drinking buddy, but like a man wants a woman. In his bed...riding her hard...touching and tasting every inch of her body.

If he didn't move now, he'd be in the same way he'd been all those months ago. But, this time, he couldn't blame his desire on alcohol.

He moved, with the good intention of leaving the bed. However, before he could get to the edge, Fiona's leg slid over his and hooked around the back. She shifted closer, placing her sex against the top of his thigh.

Duncan swallowed a groan and tried to untangle himself from her arms and legs without waking her.

As he moved her arm, his knuckles brushed against her breast.

She caught his wrist and pressed his palm to one rounded orb.

The nipple hardened into a tight little bud, perfect for tasting. If she'd been awake and fully capable of granting permission for him to slake his lust with her body, he'd be all over her.

Holy hell, he was in trouble and couldn't seem to get out of it. The more he tried to ease her off of him, the more she slipped past his efforts and established another stronghold.

When her eyes opened and looked up at him in the dim light, he knew he'd lost the battle. "Hey," he said.

Her face was close enough he only had to move it an inch or two to press his lips to her forehead.

"Hey." She stretched, her body rubbing against his. "Am I crowding you?"

"Uh. No. But maybe I should go to the other room," he said softly, brushing a strand of her fiery hair from her cheek.

She leaned into his hand. "Do you want to?"

He chuckled, his body so hard and tight he could barely breathe. "Want to what? Want to kiss the freckle on the tip of your nose? Yes. Want to nibble on your ear lobe? Uh-huh. Want to taste your breasts, one at a time? Definitely. Want to get naked and make love to you? Oh, hell yeah." He shook his head. "Should I? Probably not. Will I?" He drew in a deep breath and let it go slowly. "Well, now, that would be totally up to you." He leaned up on his elbow and stared down at her. "The question is...what do *you* want?"

Her cheeks had blossomed a deeper pink with each word he'd uttered. "I want..." The tip of her tongue darted out to wet her lips. "I want all of that..." She rolled over on top of him and straddled his hips, settling her bottom on his erection. With her hands planted on his chest, she stared down into his eyes. "I want all of that and more."

Duncan gripped her hips and adjusted her seating to ease the strain on his cock. "Sweetheart, you aren't fully awake. You don't know what you want."

She pressed a finger to his mouth. "Shh. Or you'll wake the baby." Then in a quiet voice said, "I'm wide awake, and I know exactly what I want. But let me be clear, if we do all…the things you mentioned, it by no means obligates either one of us to any kind of commitment." She crossed her arms over her chest. "Agreed?"

He didn't like the sound of her proposal, but he was in no position to argue. She held all the cards and was sitting on the deck. "Agreed," he said, "But—"

She pressed her finger to his lips again. "No buts. We have a lot to accomplish before you-know-who wakes up. Let's get cracking." She leaned down and replaced her finger with her lips. Her position caused her crotch to rub over the long line of his shaft. He moaned into her mouth and dug his hand into her soft, thick hair, bringing her closer so that he could slip his tongue between her teeth and taste her.

She kissed him long and hard, caressing his tongue with hers, her body writhing against his.

Time stood still for long moments. Duncan began to wonder if he was actually still asleep, dreaming about this woman. Then she moved downward, dragging her lips over his chin and down the length of his neck. She paused at the pulse banging at the base of his throat. Her lips pressed there, and she flicked her tongue against his skin.

Fiona leaned back and tugged at the hem of his shirt, shoving it up his torso. Since he was lying on his back, it didn't get far. She leaned back and helped him sit up, and then dragged his shirt over his head and flung it against the wall.

"Hey, that's my favorite fishing shirt," he whispered.

"Go fishing another day." She pushed back against the mattress and continued her journey down his torso to the elastic waistband of his shorts.

Her fingers hooked the elastic and drew the fabric downward.

He raised his hips, allowing her to slide his shorts even lower until his cock sprang free of its confines.

Her fingers curled around his length, warm and strong.

"You sure you want to do this?" he said through gritted teeth. "Once we get started, I'm not sure I'll be able to stop."

Her grip tightened around him then loosened, sliding down his length to cup his balls. "I'm sure." She bent to run her tongue around the rim of his cock. "Are you up to this? Once I get started, I'm not sure I'll be able to stop," she said, echoing his words.

"Darlin' I've never been more certain."

She looked up and met his gaze. "No regrets?"

He frowned and wondered if she meant more by her question than what he was reading into it. "No regrets." He couldn't regret making love to Fiona. She was hot, sexy and amazing. Why had he thought she was just one of the guys for so long? There was nothing guy-ish about Fiona. She was one hundred percent woman, and he ached to be inside her.

Fiona had other ideas, equally as enticing. When she wrapped her lips around him, he struggled to keep from coming right then. She sank down over him and came back up to run her tongue over the slit.

Duncan groaned.

"Shhh," she said, her breath blowing over his heated cock.

Again she took him into her mouth and sucked him hard until he bumped against the back of her throat. Then she moved up and down, again and again, until Duncan tensed, teetering on the edge of no return. He gripped her hair and pulled her off.

"Too much?" she asked, crawling up his body to lie over his chest.

"Oh, babe. Not enough. I don't want to blow until you're there."

"I'm halfway there."

"Halfway isn't good enough. I want you to come so hard, you'll feel the vibrations into tomorrow."

"Promises, promises," she murmured as she trailed kisses across the base of his throat and up to his mouth. She tasted of him.

Duncan kissed her and rolled her onto her back. He dragged her shirt over her head and flung it over the headboard. With what little control he had left, he worked his way over her body, kissing, nipping and tonguing every inch and crevice.

He paused to lavish his attention on her sweet breasts. They were not too big, not too little, but just right. Sucking the nipple into his mouth, he pulled gently, flicking the beaded tip with the tip of his tongue.

"Mmm," she moaned softly.

"Shh," he said, blowing warm air over her damp breast. Moving to the other, he gave it the same attention as the first then worked his way down her torso to the elastic band of her bikini panties. Ever so slowly, he edged the elastic lower and lower, exposing the tuft of auburn hair covering her sex. When his patience reached its end, he slipped the panties the rest of the way down her legs and off the ends of her toes.

Duncan parted her legs and slipped between them. Parting her folds with his thumb, he blew a warm stream of air over the narrow strip of flesh, then tapped it with his tongue.

Her hips rose from the mattress, and her fingers dug into his scalp. "Yes," she breathed.

He swept his tongue across that special place and sucked it softly between his teeth.

Fiona raised her knees and dug her heels into the mattress, raising her hips to him. "Please," she begged, her head turning from side to side. "Please."

Duncan slid a finger into her slick channel, then another, until he had three inside, swirling around, preparing her for his length. But she wasn't there yet, and he wanted her to be completely mindless and ready for him when he came inside her.

Pumping his fingers in and out of her, he claimed her clit once again, laving, sucking and swirling his tongue around that nerve-packed knot of magic.

Fiona arched off the bed, her body tense, her fingernails digging into his skin. Then she froze, her breathing arrested, her body held so very tight.

Her hips bucked once, and she gasped. They bucked again, and she let go of the breath she'd been holding and hooked his shoulders with her hands, dragging him up her body.

Once he was poised at her entrance, she stopped pulling and reversed thrusters.

"Wait," she whispered urgently.

"Babe, I'm not sure I can." He was so hard and tight, he'd ache through the night if she called a halt now.

"Protection," she said softly.

Holy hell, he was about to commit the same mistake he'd made the first time he'd made love to her. He pushed away from her and leaned over the side of the bed to where he'd dropped his jeans after he'd showered. Fumbling for the pocket and the wallet he'd left inside, he prayed he had what he needed. If not…what sweet hell he'd be in that night. His fingers closed around the wallet, he ripped it out of the pocket and came up on the bed, digging through the pockets until his fingers closed around salvation.

He pulled it out and flung the wallet. It hit the wall with a thud and slid to the floor.

Fiona froze, her gaze going to the crib.

Duncan's followed, his breath lodging in his throat.

Through the railing, they could see Caity moving.

When she stilled, he let go of the breath he'd held, ripped open the packet and rolled the condom over his shaft, his entire body shaking with his need to hurry.

Resuming the same position he'd held a moment before, he paused with his cock at her entrance, his gaze pinning hers. "Are you still with me?"

She nodded, gripped his hips and brought him home, raising her bottom off the bed to meet him halfway.

She felt so good, her channel wrapping around him, slick, and incredibly hot.

Past his ability to take it slow, he pulled out and pressed back into her. "I'm not going to last long."

"Don't hold back. I'm ready," she said.

Duncan pumped in and out of her, again and again until he thrust one last time, launching over the edge and blasting into the stratosphere. For a long time, he remained buried inside her, his cock throbbing against her channel, his body tense.

When he returned to earth, he dropped down on

her and rolled with her to their sides. He rested for a long moment, catching his breath before he leaned close and pressed a kiss to her forehead, each of her eyelids and, finally, her mouth.

"That was incredible," he said.

"As good as the first time?" she asked.

"Better. My wits weren't dulled by alcohol." He shook his head. "I'm sorry I was such an ass back then. You deserved better."

"I can't regret what created Caity," she said.

"About the no commitment clause…" he said.

Movement in the crib captured Fiona's attention. She moved, releasing him from inside her. "We need to dress."

"We need to talk."

Caity grunted, her arms and legs kicking at the blanket around her.

Fiona reached for her night shirt and pulled it over her head. Then she rolled out of the bed onto her feet.

Caity grunted louder and let out a whimpering cry.

Fiona stood beside the crib, patting her back.

When that didn't help and Caity continued to fuss, Fiona lifted her into her arms and carried her to the rocking chair.

Duncan rose and dressed in his shorts and T-shirt. "Want me to rock her so you can sleep?"

She shook her head. "She's probably out of sorts with so many changes and new people around her."

Caity settled against her mother's chest, laying her cheek against Fiona's heart.

As they rocked, the baby quieted, her eyelids closing, the crescents of her lashes making dark half-circles against her cheeks.

Watching the two of them, so close and perfect, made Duncan's heart hurt. Already, he loved his little girl more than life itself. And he'd always loved Fiona. He just hadn't known it until that night fifteen months ago.

Then why the hell had he waited so long to do anything about it?

She had no reason to believe him if he said he loved her now. Fiona was a proud and independent woman. She would hate to think he'd marry her only because of the baby.

Hell, he'd made a mess of their lives. Somehow, he had to fix it.

But how?

"I'm going to leave you two alone, for now, but I'm only down the hall. All you have to do is call my name, and I'll be there," he said. "Unless you want me to stay?" He prayed she'd tell him he could stay.

"No," she said. "We'll be all right. You might as well get some sleep."

"I'll be in later to take over so that you can sleep."

"No need. Once she's fully asleep, I'll put her in

her crib and go to bed myself." She tipped her chin toward the door. "Go. Sleep. And don't worry. We agreed. No commitment."

With his marching orders in hand, Duncan walked out of the room and down the hall to his mother's sewing room, his fists clenched. He wanted to go right back into Fiona's room and tell her he wasn't going anywhere. He was staying with them... forever. So she should just get used to it.

But he couldn't. He had some lost time to make up with Fiona. And he'd better get it right this time or risk losing her.

And he couldn't lose her. Fiona was his life. He'd missed her all those months and grieved the loss of her friendship and love.

He had to get her back.

CHAPTER 10

FIONA LAID awake halfway through the night, partly because she'd been working nights and hadn't fully adjusted to sleeping at night, but mostly because she'd done it again.

She'd seduced Duncan McKinnon. Hell, she'd practically thrown herself at him. Thankfully, she'd had the mental wherewithal to insist on protection. All she needed was to get pregnant, again.

In a perfect world, where Duncan loved her, she'd welcome another pregnancy, or two or three. She'd love to have four children with dark hair and green eyes like the McKinnons. But she refused to trap Duncan in a marriage he didn't want.

All Fiona's life, she'd sworn she wouldn't have just one child. Life as an only child had been lonely. Especially after her parents had passed away.

She'd hung around the McKinnon family because

they were the family she'd wished she'd had. They were close-knit and there for each other.

They'd proven their devotion all over again by coming home when their father disappeared. The entire family rallied around each other when the going got tough.

When she finally fell asleep, her dreams were erotic, with she and Duncan lying naked in the summer sun or next to a stream or in the Montana moonlight. Always naked, bodies entwined and filled with fiery passion. Twice, she'd woken in the early hours of the morning, feeling as if the dreams had been real. When she'd reached out to touch him, the bed beside her was empty.

Her heart pinched a little harder each time with her disappointment.

Near sunrise, she fell into a deep sleep and slept well into the morning. When she opened her eyes, the sun was shining around the curtains covering the windows.

She sat up with a jerk, her gaze shooting toward the baby crib.

It was empty. Caity and her blanket were missing.

Her heart pounding hard against her ribs, Fiona leaped out of bed, pulled on a pair of jeans and a T-shirt and ran out on the landing.

The sound of a baby's giggles reached from the floor below.

The tightness in her chest eased, and she let out a sigh.

Hurrying back into the bedroom, she grabbed her toiletries and crossed the hallway to the bathroom. For the next few minutes, she worked to tame her hair into a loose messy bun on the crown of her head and applied a little makeup. Not that she was very good at it, but she needed to look good when she faced Duncan.

She had to be strong in the face of heartbreak. Because when it came to Duncan, he broke her heart without even trying.

Fiona didn't have time for a broken heart. She had a life to live and a child to raise.

Back in her room, she put on a pair of boots and changed from the T-shirt to a button-up green blouse that she'd been told emphasized the green in her eyes.

Feeling a little more put together, she headed down the stairs to the ground floor where she found Molly playing with Caity on the floor of the living room.

Mrs. McKinnon entered the room with a smile on her face. "I hope you don't mind. I was up early and ducked my head into your room to see if our little bundle of joy was awake." She grinned at her grand-daughter. "She was stirring, and her eyes were open, so I brought her down here, gave her a bottle and changed her diaper. I thought you could use some sleep."

"I guess I needed it," Fiona said. "Thank you."

"I have breakfast warming in the oven for you. The others have all eaten and have been out in the barn for the past couple of hours. Take your time. Duncan said he'd be ready to go whenever you are."

"Go?" Fiona's brow furrowed.

"He figured you'd want to visit the Faulkners this morning, first thing." Mrs. McKinnon's lips pressed into a thin line. "I hope they don't give you any trouble."

So, Duncan was outside, and he'd accompany her to the Faulkners.

At least she had a few more minutes respite before she had to face the man she'd coerced into making love to her...for the second time.

"Go on, have breakfast," Molly said. "We have Caity-did under control."

Fiona entered the kitchen, checked in the oven and found a plate of food covered in foil.

She poured a glass of orange juice and carried the glass and plate to the table where she sat by herself, picking at the fluffy scrambled eggs, bacon and homemade biscuits.

The kitchen had always been the heart of the house. It was the second largest room, besides the living room, with a large, heavy wooden table, big enough for a family of seven and five guests.

Fiona had always felt welcome to sit down to dinner without being invited. Mrs. McKinnon made enough food to feed an army. With four teenage boys in the house she'd had to.

Though she'd sat alone at the table in her little rented house, she'd never been alone at a table in the McKinnon house. Being alone now felt strange and a little depressing.

Mrs. McKinnon entered the kitchen with her usual smile, carrying Caity. "Do you think she can have some of her baby food? She had a bottle earlier, but I think she's ready for more."

"Absolutely," Fiona said. "She's really taken a liking to the carrots and peas."

Mrs. McKinnon settled Caity in the high chair next to where Fiona sat at the table and buckled her in. Molly drifted in, poured a cup of coffee and brought it over to sit by Fiona.

And just like that, Fiona wasn't alone anymore.

For the next half an hour, the women talked about baby food, learning to walk and the best age for a child to learn to ride a horse.

Caity ate carrots and got more on her than in her in the process.

The atmosphere was light, fun and happy.

Fiona was smiling when Duncan walked through the door.

Immediately, her smile faded, and she looked

away, suddenly shy and feeling awkward in his presence.

"Oh, good. You're awake. We can make that trip out to the Faulkners' place whenever you're ready."

Fiona stood and carried her plate to the sink.

"I'll take care of the dishes," Mrs. McKinnon said.

"And we have Caity for the day," Molly added. "You two have fun at the Faulkners'." Her lips twisted in a wry grin. "Try not to get shot."

"We'll do our best," Duncan said. "If we're not back by nightfall, send out a posse."

His mother shook her head. "Don't say such things, Duncan McKinnon. With your father missing, I couldn't stand it if one of my boys was next."

Duncan hugged his mother. "Sorry, Mom. We'll be fine, and we'll be back before nightfall, or I'll call and let you know otherwise."

She patted her son's face. "You're a good son. Be sure to take care of Fiona. Don't let those Faulkner boys treat her badly."

"I won't." He lifted his chin toward Fiona. "Ready?"

She nodded. "I just have to grab my wallet with my badge in it."

"I thought you were on leave," Duncan reminded her.

"Yeah, but it doesn't hurt to remind them that, on leave or not, I still work for the sheriff's department."

Duncan shook his head. "A badge never stopped a

Faulkner from being an ass or committing a crime, but maybe it will this time."

Fiona snorted softly. Duncan was probably right. "At the very least, it'll give us one more thing to nail them on if they try anything stupid, knowing they're doing it to an officer of the law."

She ran up to her room, grabbed the thin wallet she kept in her back pocket, her shoulder holster, gun and jacket. When she had everything in place, she ran back down the stairs.

Molly was with Caity in the living room again. "Duncan's waiting outside."

"Thanks." She hurried across the floor, kissed Caity and gave her a quick hug. "I'll see you later. Don't give your Aunt Molly any fits."

"She and I are going to get along just fine," Molly said. "And Parker will be around if we need backup."

"Good. I'll have my cell phone and my sheriff's radio with me. I'm sure the cell phone won't work out in the hills. If you need me, contact dispatch and they can relay a call."

Molly nodded. "We'll be fine. Go."

Fiona squared her shoulders and walked out on the deck.

Duncan stood between her SUV and his truck. "Which one?"

"My SUV. It's old, and the paint is starting to fade. If it earns some buckshot holes, I won't be too unhappy." She nodded toward the truck. "Is the truck yours?"

He nodded. "Yup. When I got word about my father, I drove over from Ft. Lewis."

"I'd hate for the Faulkners to scratch, bang or destroy your truck. You always took care of your vehicles growing up." She smiled, avoiding his direct gaze. "Do you want to drive?"

"It's up to you."

When she handed him the keys, her fingers brushed against his palm in the process. A flash of electric awareness raced up her arm and downward to that aching place low in her belly.

She was sore from their lovemaking, but it was a delicious kind of sore. Every move she made reminded her of how wonderful it had been. Too bad it could never happen again. Though he'd been willing, it didn't mean anything to him. He'd agreed to the no commitment clause she'd offered up front. What had she expected? A man who was even mildly interested in a woman wasn't going to say no to an offer of sex with no strings attached.

Fiona climbed into the passenger seat and secured her seatbelt over her lap.

Duncan slipped in behind the steering wheel and adjusted the seat to allow for his longer legs. He started the SUV and drove down the long drive to the highway.

"We'll need to stop at the sheriff's department on

the way through town. Sheriff Barron might've already gone out to the Faulkners'."

Duncan nodded and picked up speed on the highway headed into Eagle Rock.

Silence hung like a heavy fog inside the SUV for the first couple of miles.

Duncan cleared his throat. "Want to talk about last night?"

Fiona stared out the side window, keeping her face averted but watching him in the reflection off the glass. "No."

"We need to."

"Why?" she asked. "What happened was no big deal. We both agreed it didn't mean anything."

Duncan frowned. "I didn't agree to that."

"Sorry," she said. "We agreed to no commitment. I'm okay with that."

"What if I'm not?" Duncan asked, shooting a glance her way.

They were nearing Eagle Rock and would be stopping at the sheriff's department momentarily.

"Look, can we not talk about this now? We have more than enough to think about with your father missing and someone threatening my family."

Duncan's mouth firmed into a thin line. "Okay, for now, but we will talk...today."

Fiona gave brief nod. "Fine," she said, though fine wasn't fine. She didn't want to talk. The more they talked, the sooner he'd get around to saying he wanted to be a part of Caity's life—not hers.

He might even make an offer of marriage, which she'd have to turn down. He wasn't in love with her. Duncan would be marrying her to be with his daughter.

What they'd had last night wasn't love. It had been raw, unfettered sex. Nothing more.

Then why was the thought of only one night with Duncan ripping her apart from the inside?

She wanted so much more.

As soon as Duncan pulled to a stop in front of the sheriff's office, Fiona jumped out and hurried inside.

Duncan walked alongside her, his eyes slightly narrowed as if he was trying to figure out what the hell was wrong with her.

Well, there was a lot wrong with her. She'd fallen in love with her best friend, and he didn't feel the same.

CHAPTER 11

DUNCAN WANTED TO GRAB FIONA, wrap her in his arms and kiss her senseless. But he couldn't understand what was going through her head. Did she really believe he didn't want commitment? Or was it that she didn't love him and wanted to remain single? Hell, had she found someone else she loved and wanted to marry?

The thought knifed him in the gut.

Fiona hadn't mentioned that she had another man in her life. She'd called *him* when her house had been burglarized. Granted, he had the most at stake of any man when it came to dealing with Fiona. She had his baby.

Fiona had come with him to the Iron Horse Ranch instead of calling someone else to ask for a place to stay. But had that been because he'd been so insistent? Or because of the baby?

Questions whirled in his mind as he followed her through the door.

"Guthrie, you really don't know how to be off duty, do you?" Sheriff Barron said from inside his office.

"Not when I'm being threatened, and then the man who threatens me turns up dead." She stopped in front of his desk and braced her hands on her hips. "Any news?"

"The coroner stayed up through the night examining the body." The sheriff leaned back in his desk chair. "Wally was pretty banged up, and his chest was crushed. All injuries were consistent with him being hit by a vehicle and run over several times."

Fiona winced. "The bastard trashed my house and threw knives at me, but I wouldn't wish such a violent death on anyone."

Duncan could, but he didn't voice his opinion.

"His shirt was ripped as if it had been snagged on something. I'm wondering if it was caught on the front bumper of the vehicle that hit him."

"We're headed out to the Faulkners' place this morning," Fiona said. "I'll see what I can find."

The sheriff shook his head. "I have to transport a prisoner to Bozeman this morning. I don't suppose you'd wait until I get back to check in with the Faulkners?"

Fiona's jaw hardened. "The more time they have,

the more likely they'll destroy the evidence. It's a pattern with them."

The sheriff pushed back from his desk and stood, his face grim. "One other thing you need to know before you head out there."

"What's that?"

"Since the evidence has gone missing, we had nothing to hold Mark Faulkner in jail. He was released from Bozeman this morning."

Fiona cursed. "How did they find out the flashlight was missing?"

The sheriff shrugged. "I assume whoever took it informed the district attorney. They called this morning to verify. I couldn't lie. It's gone, and the state is sending an investigator out to find out how we could've let evidence walk out of our office."

"Great. And how long before the press gets hold of this and calls us incompetent?" Fiona shook her head. "Not that I'm calling you incompetent. But the press loves shit like this."

"Eagle Rock is so far off the radar, I can't imagine anyone caring," Duncan said.

"I hope you're right," the sheriff said. He turned to Fiona. "Do you have your gun?"

She opened her jacket, displaying her weapon in its holster.

"Good. Normally, I wouldn't give this advice, but if you even *think* you're in danger, shoot first and ask questions later." He faced Duncan. "I assume you're going with her?"

Duncan nodded. "I am."

"Same goes for you. The Faulkners don't play by anyone's rules but their own. They fancy themselves as survivalists and swear their property is a free nation and not subject to U.S. or Montana laws." The sheriff shook his head. "Maybe I should let Guthrie take the prisoner, so I can go up to the Faulkner place."

"I'm off duty, remember," Fiona said. "You said so yourself. Besides, I'd go anyway."

"I should fire you." The sheriff pushed a hand through his gray hair. "But I can't get any better help."

Fiona grinned. "I'll take that as a compliment."

"Wasn't meant as one," Sheriff Barron grumbled, "Look, just be careful. I need you in the department in one piece. Can't afford to carry you on workers comp until you recover from whatever injuries they might inflict."

"I'll be with her," Duncan reiterated.

"Yeah," the sheriff's eyes narrowed, "but there are a lot more of them than there are of the two of you."

As Fiona and Duncan walked toward the exit, the door opened and Missy Drennan entered, carrying a big, covered basket. When she saw them, her eyes widened for a moment before she relaxed and smiled. "Duncan. It's so nice to see you home." She turned to Fiona, her eyes narrowing slightly. "Hi

Fiona. I thought you weren't working for the next couple of days?"

"Hey, Missy," Fiona said. "I'm not working. I just stopped by to talk to the sheriff."

Missy leaned to the right, looking past Fiona. "Where's my sweet Caity? Did you bring her with you?"

Fiona shook her head. "Not today. I have some errands to run. She's out at Iron Ranch with her..." she hesitated for a moment, before finishing, "grandmother and Aunt Molly."

Missy shot a glance between Fiona and Duncan. "I heard about that," she said in a whisper. "I bet you were surprised to know you had a baby girl."

Duncan's teeth clamped hard. It still hurt that Fiona hadn't told him about the baby sooner. He forced a smile to his lips. "I'm thrilled. She's a beautiful baby, and I'm enjoying getting to know her."

Missy's gaze saddened. "Fiona's so lucky to have her. Cole and I have been trying for the past three years to have a baby, but so far, we've not been blessed. We're hoping to do the fertility treatments once we get enough money to start. We've been saving."

Fiona touched Missy's arm. "I'll keep you and Cole in my prayers."

"Thank you. In the meantime, hug Caity for me and have a cookie." She smiled widely, held open the basket and raised a dishtowel to display at least two dozen cookies. "They're chocolate chip."

Ellen stuck her head out the door of her office. "Did I hear cookies?" She came out of her office with her headset on. "Oatmeal raisin like you brought a couple of days ago?"

"No," Missy said. "This time I brought chocolate chip."

"Even better." Ellen hurried forward. "I'm starving."

"Do you want me to run over to the Blue Moose Tavern and get you some real food?" Missy offered.

Ellen shook her head, making her short blond curls bounce. "No, thank you. I brought a sandwich, but I needed something to tide me over until lunch." She fished a couple of the cookies out of the basket and started to pop one into her mouth. She hit the mic on her headset and knocked the foam cover off. It bounced on the floor and rolled between a file cabinet and the wall.

"Shoot," Ellen said and bent to retrieve the cover. "That's the third time I've done that this week." She reached her fingers between the cabinet and the wall but couldn't quite reach it. "My fingers are too short and fat. Anything around here I can use to fish that out?"

"Wait," Missy said. "I have a file in my purse." She set the basket on a desk and dug into her voluminous purse, fishing for a few seconds before she unearthed a thin, metal file. "This should do it." She squatted beside Ellen, slid the file into the gap and flicked it, sending the microphone cover out like a shot. "There." She slid the file back into her purse and straightened.

"You're a lifesaver," Ellen blew the dust off the foam and slid it over the microphone on her headset.

"I'm pretty good with tight spaces," Missy said. "I used to work in a microchip factory when I lived in Denver. I haven't worked since I married Cole and moved to Eagle Rock. There aren't that many jobs here, unless I want to be a waitress at the diner or the Blue Moose." She shrugged and dropped the file into the basket. "We keep hoping we'll have a family for me to raise. That'll keep me busy."

"I'll keep my fingers crossed for you," Ellen said. "And thank you for the cookies."

"I'll leave the basket with you this time and collect it later," Missy said.

"Are you going to bring cookies every other day on a regular basis?" Ellen asked, raising her eyebrows. "I could get used to it. And I could get fat, too."

Fiona snorted. "I think you could eat your weight in ice cream and not gain an ounce."

Duncan studied Ellen. She was thin with short, curly blond hair and freckles across her nose. She looked like she could use a fully loaded cheeseburger or two.

Ellen shrugged. "I don't have to worry too much. Yet. But I'm sure the older I get the more I'll spread." She waved a cookie. "In the meantime, cookies are great. Gotta go, got a call coming in." She pressed the button on the side of her headset as she walked back to her office, talking to the person on the other end of the call.

"She's always been a tiny woman," Duncan noted. "In high school she was voted most likely to slip through a crack in the sidewalk."

Fiona smiled. "Ellen's great. Did you know her husband died of cancer a year ago?"

Duncan shook his head. "Bill Ledbetter died?" How'd he miss that bit of news from home? It must have happened while he was deployed. His mother had written and called when she could, but she hadn't mentioned Bill's passing. "He was a good guy. Always setting the curve in class. The man was smart. What kind of cancer did he die of?"

"Brain tumor," Missy said. "It was so sad. They were planning on having a family. They saved some of his sperm. I think Ellen might try to have his baby when she's ready."

Duncan's brow rose. He'd never heard of someone doing that. Ellen must have loved her husband deeply to want to go through pregnancy and raise their baby all by herself.

"Thank you for the cookies, Missy." Fiona plucked two from the basket and headed for the door. "We'd better get out there before another murder weapon disappears."

Missy followed them out the door. "Murder weapon?" she asked.

Fiona gave her a brief smile but ignored her question. "Good luck with the fertility treatments, Missy."

"Oh, those won't happen until we save a lot more money." Missy sighed. "I hope that will be soon."

Duncan dipped his head. "Missy, have a good day." He followed Fiona out to the SUV and held the driver's door for her.

She frowned up at him and hesitated getting into the vehicle. "I thought you were driving?"

"Changed my mind," he said and waited for her to get in. Then he closed the door and walked around to get into the passenger seat. After he buckled his belt, he reached beneath his jacket and pulled out his hand gun. With a click, he released the magazine, checked that it was fully loaded and shoved it back into the handle. When he looked up, he realized they hadn't moved from the parking space. His gaze met hers. "What?"

"Preparing for war?" she asked, a smile quirking the corners of her lips.

Her cocky look and the hint of mirth took him back to their high school days. "Have I ever told you that you have a beautiful smile?"

To his disappointment, her smile disappeared. "No."

"Then I'm sorry I've been neglectful in that respect. I remember you smiling a lot more back in the day."

She shifted into gear, her lips thinning into a straight line. "I had a lot more to smile about, back then."

"And you don't now...?" His gaze never wavered from her, but she wasn't meeting his with her own.

"No. Except for Caity. My world revolves around her. It's a lot of responsibility, raising a baby and keeping her safe from harm." She held up a hand. "Not that I resent the responsibility. It's just that it weighs heavily on me. Every decision I make has to take her welfare into account. She's dependent on me for everything. If I die..."

"Caity has an entire family of McKinnons to look out for her. But you're right. She needs her mother." He stared at the road ahead, his gun in his lap. "Are you sure you want to confront the Faulkners?"

Fiona nodded. "I have to believe they won't out and out shoot me."

"If you find what you're looking for, will you make the arrest?"

"I had hoped I could say yes. But if we find the vehicle that hit Wally, how will I know who was driving it? And without a warrant, I can't confiscate."

Duncan nodded. "They're not going to give up the murderer."

"All we know is that it wasn't Mark. He wasn't released until this morning."

"Which means we have two murderers running loose in the county now." Duncan sighed. "I used to think Eagle Pass and this county would be a great place to raise kids. We had fun and were fairly safe growing up."

"Times have changed," Fiona said.

"Or we're old enough now to recognize bad eggs in a community."

"I think you've got that right. Seems the Faulkners were pulling crap even back when we were kids."

"Yeah. Beau was busted a couple times for possession with intent to sell drugs to the residents of the reservation."

"I remember. He's still up to his same old tricks."

"What's Tripp up to now?" Duncan asked.

"He's running a whore house." Fiona snorted. "Or rather a whore trailer outside a biker bar on the county line. I think he listens to the police radio, because every time we go out to bust them, they've cleared out."

"I'm surprised their mama's still alive," Duncan commented.

"She rules with an iron fist." Fiona drove out of Eagle Rock, headed for Cooter's Bluff and the Faulkner compound.

"As much as those boys push others around, you'd think they'd want to be in charge."

"Barb won't let them, as long as she's alive and breathing," Fiona said.

"My point, exactly."

Fiona gripped the steering wheel tightly as she entered a curve in the highway. "I guess they're too afraid that if they shoot at her, they'll miss. I wouldn't put it past Barb to kill her own sons if they crossed her."

"That kind of childrearing isn't conducive to well-rounded, well-behaved adults."

Fiona laughed. "No kidding."

Thirty minutes later, Fiona turned off the highway onto a gravel road leading up into the hills.

The rutted path twisted through a forest of lodge-pole pine trees and climbed upward.

When Duncan thought they couldn't get any deeper into the sticks, the forest opened to a clearing filled with a conglomeration of buildings and shacks. Scattered between them were the rusting remains of old tractors and trucks, stacks of rotting wooden pallets, concrete blocks, more junk and trash.

At the center was a log cabin with a wide front porch. The logs were a weathered gray, showing no signs of having been treated since they'd been erected into a house.

As Fiona pulled to a stop in the middle of the compound, men emerged from neighboring shacks and the log cabin. Each carried guns of varying shapes and sizes—shot guns, rifles, semi-automatic rifles and pistols resting in holsters on jean-clad hips.

For a moment, Duncan felt as though they'd stepped onto the set of a spaghetti western movie in the shootout scene. A lump of unease settled in the pit of his belly. "Maybe we should turn around and head back down the mountain," he said.

Fiona swallowed, the muscles in her throat working hard. After drawing in a deep breath, she squared her shoulders and pushed open the door. "I'm here for answers."

Mark Faulkner stood at the top of the steps to the porch. "You're trespassing." He held a shotgun in his hands. "Leave, or I'll shoot."

"Mark, you're in enough trouble already for murder, you might as well put that shotgun away before you hurt yourself," Fiona said.

Mark glared and shifted his weapon to his other hand. "What's the matter Guthrie? Too afraid of us to come out on your own?"

Fiona lifted her chin and stared into Mark's eyes. "You don't scare me, Mark. It won't be long before we put you away for life for murdering Clay Bennett and Wally Bing."

"I don't know what you're talking about," Mark said. "And you're still trespassing." He raised his weapon to his shoulder. "You gonna leave, or am I gonna have to claim that I felt I was in danger and had to shoot?"

Fiona raised her hands. "Guess you'll have to shoot. I'm not leaving until I have answers."

"What kind of answers are you looking for, girl?" The heavyset Barb Faulkner, pushed through the men crowded onto the front porch. "Fiona Guthrie, how the heck are you?"

Fiona gave a polite nod. "Good, Mrs. Faulkner. Only I'd be a lot better if your people hadn't sent someone out to hurt me and defile my house. Know anything about that?"

Barb's eyes narrowed. "Why do you think we had anything to do with it?"

Fiona's gaze swept the menagerie of vehicles. She stopped at the largest, a monster truck with over-sized tires and a jacked-up suspension. "I had word Wally Bing worked for you."

Barb stared at Fiona. "He did."

Fiona ambled toward the big truck, still talking. Duncan followed, his attention moving from one Faulkner to another. They circled around him and Fiona, closing them in.

He didn't like that their escape route had been cut off. Duncan kept his jacket loose, his hands free and ready to dive for the weapon beneath his arm. He'd have to be quick and ready to drop and roll, or they'd cut him down first.

Drawing his weapon first would be a huge mistake at this point. If they shot him, that would leave Fiona unprotected.

He wished he'd convinced her to wait until they could bring the Montana Army National Guard as backup. The Faulkners weren't going to turn over any of their own. Not without a fight.

"And Wally was working for you when he trashed my house and wrote your message on my wall." She didn't ask. She squared off with Barb and crossed her arms over her chest.

Barb planted her hands on her hips. "I don't know what you're talking about."

"Wally didn't have any reason to tell me to keep my mouth shut." She tipped her head toward Mark who still held his shotgun to his shoulder, aimed at her. "Mark, however, has a shit-ton of reasons, namely fifty years to life for committing murder."

Duncan tensed and moved to stand between Mark and Fiona.

"Why you—" The murderer shifted his hold on the shotgun.

His mother raised her hand and brought the shotgun down to point at the porch, not Fiona. "You got a lot of nerve comin' out here without a search warrant, accusin' me and mine of murderin' Wally Bing when we were here all night playin' poker. I got witnesses who can attest to that fact." She glanced around at the men surrounding them. "Don't I?"

By the time Barb finished speaking, Fiona had reached the front of the jacked-up pickup with a dent in the front bumper and a piece of fabric hanging off a ragged piece of metal.

Duncan could see what she'd been looking for, and he held his breath.

"Did I say I was here about Wally Bing's murder?" Fiona raised an eyebrow.

"Why else are you out here harassing us?" Barb demanded.

"Any reason why I should think you had anything to do with Wally's death?" Fiona asked, her voice dead even. "He had to mean something to you. He worked for you. Or had he misspelled your intended message on the wall of my bedroom or done something else to warrant being run over by a pickup with knobby tires, not once, but several times?"

"It's time for you to leave." Tripp Faulkner stepped up behind Fiona before Duncan could get between them.

"Move away from the deputy," Duncan said.

"We ain't got no gripe with the McKinnons," Barb said. "Leave my boy alone."

"I will when he moves away from the deputy," Duncan said, his fists clenching.

"I can handle this," Fiona said. She'd tensed and was ready to do battle, but Tripp had seventy to one hundred pounds on her, and she had her back to him.

He made a grab for her, hooking his arm around her neck.

In the blink of an eye, Fiona elbowed the man in

the gut, slipped beneath his elbow and yanked his arm up behind his back, pushing it hard between his shoulder blades.

"Bitch!" he yelled.

"You attacked me. I defended myself. What did you expect?" When he tried to jerk himself free, Fiona pushed the arm up higher until Tripp stood on his toes to ease the pain.

"Duncan McKinnon, you best get your woman in order," Barb called out.

Duncan held up his hands. "Seems to me you need to get your son in order. All I witnessed was a woman being attacked and defending herself. Like she said." And he was damned proud of her.

One more reason to love Fiona and want her in his life forever.

With the Faulkners surrounding them at gunpoint, that forever wasn't looking like it would last for long.

CHAPTER 12

ADRENALINE RACED through Fiona's veins as she held Tripp's arm behind his back. "Are you going to behave yourself if I let you go?"

He snorted. "I'm gonna knock some manners into you, bitch."

"Like you knock the women around you employ in the trailer by Biker Hell?" Fiona said.

"I don't know what you're talking about," Tripp gritted out.

She shoved his arm up higher.

"Damn it, bitch. That hurts," he cried.

"Is that what those women say when you throw them around and punch them in the face?" She sneered at him. "Real men don't hit women. What's that make you?"

"Bitch," he spit out.

"That's right. You're a bitch." Fiona shoved up his

arm again, planted her foot the middle of his back and pushed him hard, sending him sprawling in the dirt at his brother Beau's feet.

"Hey, you can't do that to my brother." Beau stepped toward her and aimed his shotgun at her chest.

A flash of fear ripped through her. The man's glazed eyes were a good indication he was high.

Before Beau could manage to pull the trigger, Duncan cocked his leg and hit the Faulkner brother's arm in a sweeping sidekick.

Beau's finger pulled as the shotgun swung wide. The blast jerked Beau's arm back hard, and he dropped the weapon.

A man standing by another truck doubled over. "Damn, Beau," he wheezed. "You shot me."

Beau grabbed his arm and moaned. "I think you broke my arm."

"What the hell?" Duncan lunged for Beau, grabbed his hand and tried to yank the ring off his finger. "That's my father's ring!"

Beau pulled back, clenching his hand into a fist. "Get the hell away from me, McKinnon."

Duncan grabbed the man's injured arm, pulled it up behind his back then pressed his gun to Beau's temple. "Give me the goddamn ring."

Every gaze turned to Duncan and weapons pointed that way.

It all happened so fast, Fiona didn't have time to think.

Tripp had just risen from the ground and wiped the dust from his hands.

Fiona did the only thing she could think to do. She yanked up Tripp's arm back behind his back and pressed her gun to his head. "Any one of you think you're going to shoot me or Duncan, think twice. I'll put a bullet through Tripp's head and then one through yours. Got it?" Her gaze met Barb's. "Your call, Mrs. Faulkner. You willing to risk the lives of your sons?"

She glared at Fiona. Finally, she said, "Give him the ring, Beau."

"It's mine," Beau said. "I got it from a pawn shop."

His mother descended the steps and marched over to where Duncan held Beau at gunpoint. Then she held out her hand. "Give it to me." When he didn't move, she smacked him upside his head. "Beau Francis Faulkner," she said in a threatening tone.

Beau held out his hand and uncurled his fist.

His mother slid the ring from his finger and handed it to Duncan. "Now, put down your weapons," she said, her gaze going from Duncan to Fiona, and then to the men standing all around her. "All of you. Put down your guns."

The dozen or so men standing around lowered their weapons but held them at the ready.

Fiona loosened her hold on Tripp and stepped out

of his reach. She still held her gun in her hand but pointed at the ground. If anyone dared raise their weapon, she was fast enough to take them down. She'd practiced at the range so many times, she was good. Really good.

Duncan retained his hold on Beau and closed his fingers around the ring. "Where did you get this?"

"I don't remember," he said.

"Then you better start remembering soon. Where did you get it?"

"Tell him," his mother said.

"I got it from that pawn shop down in Bozeman."

"Which pawn shop in Bozeman?" Duncan pulled on Beau's arm, making the man flinch.

"Damn, that hurts! The one by the tattoo parlor," Beau said. "And that's the truth."

"It had better be, or I'll be back to beat the truth out of you." Duncan shoved him away and stared down at the ring in his palm. "My father never took off this ring."

Barb Faulkner met Duncan's gaze squarely. "My boys may have done some stupid things, but they are not in any way involved with the disappearance of your father." She poked her finger at him. "Got that?"

Duncan's eyes narrowed. "I hope you're right. Because if they are involved, I'll find them, and I'll make them wish they'd never heard the name McKinnon." He held her gaze for a long moment, and then spoke again, "And if anyone dares to threaten

Miss Guthrie or her baby again, I'll find you and make you wish you hadn't. Got that?" He glared at every man standing in the yard and on the porch. Then he held out his hand to Fiona.

She took his in hers, glad for the warmth in the icy surroundings. They backed away, then walked to her SUV. Before she got into the vehicle, she looked over the top of the door and said, "We know Mark murdered Clay Bennett. When we find the flashlight he beat him with, we'll be back."

She sank into the driver's seat, started the engine and drove out of the compound with her gaze checking her rearview mirror again and again. She was ready to duck if they started shooting at her retreating vehicle.

Bullets didn't fly. They made it out of the compound, down the long dirt road and out onto the highway.

"The big truck had a dent in the bumper and a piece of the fabric caught on some jagged metal," Fiona said.

"You're not going back there. Not without sufficient backup."

Her teeth clamped down hard and ground together. Duncan was right. She'd been so set on arresting the people who'd put Wally up to trashing her house that she hadn't thought about her own safety, or Duncan's. Things could have gone a whole lot worse than they had. That shotgun blast could have cut her down and left Caity motherless. "Thank you for deflecting Beau's aim."

Duncan nodded. "That man was high on something."

Fiona sighed. "Beau's always high on something. And high or drunk, he's belligerent."

"Being high and carrying a loaded gun is a bad combination."

"It is."

Duncan held out his hand and opened his fist. "This is my father's ring. He wore it, always. I'll bet he was wearing it the day he disappeared."

"Let's get back to the sheriff's office. I want to work on getting a warrant to confiscate that truck. And we can get someone to make a visit to that pawn shop in Bozeman."

"I'll send my brothers down there. So far, this is the only clue we've had since my father disappeared. It has to be something we can use. Something that can lead us to where he's being held."

Fiona prayed it would be the key to finding James McKinnon. The family needed him to come home safely.

Meanwhile, she needed to bring some murderers to justice.

Thankfully, the events had taken her mind off what had happened the night before. If only for a little while. As they drove toward Eagle Rock, Fiona turned over everything in her mind from the truck that had the fabric and dent to the message on the wall, to the missing flashlight.

She knew the Faulkners were behind the murders of Clay Bennett and Wally Bing. Once again, there wasn't enough evidence to nail them. Even if they confiscated the truck, anyone could have been driving it. Fiona had seen more than one of the Faulkners driving that truck on different occasions. Their fingerprints would be all over it. Short of arresting every one of the Faulkners and their minions, the sheriff's department didn't have enough on them to justify an arrest.

Fiona slammed her palm against the steering wheel, swerving close to the edge of the road. "We have to find your father. And we have to find that flashlight."

She glanced over at Duncan. He held onto the armrest, his focus on the road ahead. "You want me to drive the rest of the way?"

"No," she said and took a deep breath. "I'm just tired of people getting away with murder."

"I guess now isn't a good time to talk about last night?" he said.

When she looked over at him like he was a crazy man, she caught him smiling.

"Jerk," she muttered, but found herself lips twitching. "I can't believe you threatened to kill Beau Faulkner."

He caught her gaze briefly. "I was impressed when you put Tripp in his place."

"That bastard needs to die," she said. "I don't know how many times I've been out to the trailer by Biker Hell to stand guard while an ambulance takes one of his girls to the hospital."

"The Faulkners give humans a bad name."

"They aren't human. They're animals."

"At least we can agree on something," Duncan said. "It's a start."

"A start for what?"

He cocked an eyebrow and looked her way. "I thought we weren't talking about last night."

"Were we?"

"If you want to," he said, "I sure do."

Her fingers tightened on the steering wheel. She wasn't ready to talk about last night. What if he said he didn't want to see her again? What if he suggested they marry so that they could raise Caity together?

That would break her heart. On the flip side of her broken heart, at least she'd have him for a while. Until Caity was all grown up. Maybe in the eighteen years it took their baby to mature, they'd fall in love.

She sighed. She wasn't ready to make those kinds of decisions. Not yet. Her emotions were too raw. "I'd rather not talk about it, yet."

"Yet," he said, nodding. "But we will talk."

"We will." When she wasn't an emotional wreck.

. . .

DUNCAN HELD onto his father's ring, anxious to get back to the ranch and show his siblings and mother what he'd found at the Faulkner compound.

If Barb was telling the truth, the Faulkners had had nothing to do with his father's disappearance.

Since when had the Faulkners told the truth?

For that matter, Beau could have been lying about where he'd gotten the ring.

Duncan's fist tightened around the gold ring with the gold Iron Horse symbol overlaying a black onyx stone. "My mother gave this ring to my father for their thirtieth wedding anniversary. He'd taken her to Scotland and introduced her to his heritage that year on a two-week trip of a lifetime."

Finding the ring gave him hope of finding his father and, at the same time, made him dread finding him. The only way that ring would have come off his father's hand was if he were dead.

Fiona reached over to touch his arm. "What was it your mother always said?"

He shook his head.

"Don't borrow trouble." She squeezed his arm. "Duncan, don't give up hope. He's a strong man. He's out there somewhere. We'll find him."

He took her hand and held it in his free one, letting the warmth of her concern fill his heart. God, he loved this woman. Why had he taken so long to realize it?

He opened his mouth to tell her, but then closed it

without uttering a word. She didn't want to talk about it.

Well, she'd have to talk about it soon. He wasn't going to wait another day, another week, another year to tell her how he felt.

When she drove back into Eagle Rock, Fiona headed for the sheriff's department and parked in front of the door.

They got out and entered the office.

Ellen poked her head out of her room. "You two back so soon?"

"Yes," Fiona responded. "Did Sheriff Barron leave with the prisoner?"

Ellen nodded. "He won't be back for a couple of hours. What do you need?"

"I need a warrant to investigate the Faulkner compound."

"You'll have to work with the county judge for that. The number is in the rolodex on the sheriff's desk."

While Fiona entered the sheriff's office in search of a phone number, Duncan reached into the basket of cookies Missy had left earlier that day. He popped a cookie in his mouth and let the chocolate chips melt on his tongue. The woman was a gifted cookie baker.

When he reached in the basket for another, his hand encountering something slightly sharp and made of metal. He looked inside and found the thin metal file Missy had used to fish the microphone cover out from between the wall and cabinet.

Duncan held it up, studying it. Why would a woman carry something like that? It wasn't as if it could be used to file her nails. It was too narrow to be effective for that purpose.

Holding a cookie in one hand and the file in the other, he stepped into the sheriff's office with Fiona.

"Thank goodness the sheriff uses the old-fashioned way of storing phone numbers instead of keeping them all on the computer," she said as she sorted through a paper file on his desk in search of the judge's number. She stopped halfway through and held up a single card. "Found it." As she dialed the number, she shot a glance over at Duncan. "What's that?"

"The file Missy used earlier." He held it up higher. "Why would she carry something like this in her purse?"

"It's too narrow to be much good filing her nails."

"Exactly."

At that moment, the judge's secretary answered. Fiona told the woman that she needed a warrant to search the Faulkners' property on suspicion of vehicular manslaughter of the victim, Wally Bing.

"The judge is in court right now, but I'll be sure to

pass on the message as soon as he's out," the secretary said.

Fiona thanked her and ended the call.

Issuing a warrant would take time, especially since the judge was tied up in court. Perhaps by the time the warrant came through, the sheriff would be back, call in more deputies, and then there would be more people to go with her to confront the Faulkners. She sure as hell wasn't going back on her own. And she didn't want to risk Duncan's life again. One of them had to remain alive to raise Caity.

The thought of leaving her daughter alone in the world made Fiona's belly churn. What had she been thinking, going out to the Faulkners' place, knowing how volatile they were and without sufficient backup? Had she been harboring a death wish? Her anger over the violation of her house was inconsequential against the thought of Caity losing both parents in one visit to that den of criminals.

"Next time I decide to take on the entire Faulkner clan on their home court, remind me that I think it's a really dumb idea," she said.

Duncan laid the file on the sheriff's desk, gripped both of Fiona's arms and held her still. "Why are you saying that now?"

She stared up into his green eyes so much like hers. "My impatience nearly cost us our lives." She cupped his cheek in her palm. "Caity needs her daddy."

"She needs her mother, too," Duncan said.

Fiona nodded. "I can't believe I was so stupid. When Beau aimed that shotgun at my chest, all I could see was Caity's eyes filled with tears. She wouldn't know what had happened to her mother."

"My mother would have raised her and loved her as one of her own, if that makes you feel any better."

Her eyes filled, but she refused to let them fall. "It does help to know she would have family to take care of her, if I should die unexpectedly. Within a couple of months, she wouldn't even remember me. She'd never know that I sang her silly songs to get her to sleep. She wouldn't know how much I love her."

Duncan brushed his thumb across her cheek, capturing a tear that had managed to escape. "Don't borrow trouble, Fee. You're alive. And you're going to stay that way, if I have anything to say about it."

She laughed, the sound catching on a choked sob. "And you…you stood between me and Mark when he pointed his shotgun in my direction. Caity needs her father just as much as she needs her mother. You can't go throwing yourself in front of bullets to save me, especially when it was my stupid decision to put us both in danger. Your life is just as important as mine to Caity."

"She doesn't know me like she knows you," he said, his voice gruff.

Fiona laid her hand on Duncan's chest. "That's my fault, and I mean to correct that as soon as possible."

She stared at her hand on his chest, avoiding looking him in the eyes. "She needs to get to know her father. Every little girl needs a father to protect them, to teach them what they should expect from the boys and men in her life."

"I hope to be there for her," Duncan said, his hand cupping her face. "I want to help her learn to walk and ride a pony."

"I want that, too," she said and laid her hand over his. "She needs her daddy to be a part of her life."

"See? We can agree on more than one thing." He smiled down at her and brushed his lips across hers.

After being surrounded by the Faulkners and all their guns, Fiona realized she would rather marry Duncan, for Caity's sake, than to not marry him at all.

She stared up at him, her gaze captured by his. Her mouth opened to tell him just how much she loved him and wanted him to be a part of her life. Before she could say the words, she bit down on her bottom lip and held back all the things she wanted to say.

The problem was that she'd insisted on no commitment. How was she going to convince him that hooking up with her for the long-term would be a good idea?

She didn't know what she was going to do to make things right for their future, but she knew what she wanted right then.

Fiona leaned up on her toes and pressed her lips to Duncan's in a brief kiss. "I hope we can agree on one more thing."

He slid his lips over hers. "What's that?"

"That it feels good to kiss." She opened to him, sliding her tongue over the seam of his mouth, inviting him in.

"You're right. We can agree on that," he said and pulled her closer, deepening the kiss and sweeping his tongue across hers.

A noise in the hallway made Fiona start and pull away from Duncan right before Ellen passed the door in the hallway.

"Gotta get another one of Missy's cookies. I like the chocolate chip even better than the oatmeal raisin she brought the other day." The dispatcher passed them and continued on to the front office. She was back with a handful of cookies in seconds.

Fiona frowned and stepped out into the hallway. "Ellen, what day did Missy bring the oatmeal raisin cookies?"

Ellen tilted her head to one side and half-closed her eyes. "The day before yesterday. Cole was on duty that day. She wanted to surprise him with some freshly baked goodies." Ellen touched a hand to her headset. "Got a call coming in." She hurried back to her office, talking as she went.

Fiona faced Duncan.

He lifted the file from the sheriff's desk and stared at it. "Are you thinking what I'm thinking?"

"Maybe." She crossed to where he stood.

Duncan fit the file into the keyhole of the sheriff's desk drawer and jiggled it right and left, feeling for the locking mechanism. No matter how many times he tried, the lock didn't give.

"Let me try." Fiona took the file from him and gave it another try. Again, nothing worked.

"Maybe she didn't need his key to get into the evidence locker." Fiona carried the file down the hallway, past Ellen's office to the room they'd dedicated as the evidence locker that was a reinforced wire cage with a heavy-duty built-in lock.

She stuck the file into the lock and jiggled it in several different directions until she heard and felt a soft click.

Her breath caught in her throat, and her pulse beat faster. "Holy hell," she whispered as the cage door opened on silent hinges. The space where the flashlight had been was within easy reach. All someone had to do was grab it and go. "Holy hell," she repeated.

"Missy." Duncan shook his head. "And she had a basket big enough to carry it out without anyone noticing."

"And if Ellen was busy answering a call, she wouldn't have noticed."

"Do you think Cole knows she took it?" Duncan asked.

"I don't know." Fiona shut the cage, and the lock engaged automatically.

"Why would she take the flashlight? I wouldn't think Missy or Cole would have any connection with the Faulkners."

"Cole was the deputy who found Clay's body and the flashlight," Fiona said. "Why would he bring it in, and then steal it?"

Duncan's brow furrowed. "Maybe he didn't."

Fiona thought hard over their conversations with Cole's wife. "He probably told Missy about the flashlight." She looked up, her gaze capturing his. "Missy and Cole have been trying for years to have a baby. She said herself they were waiting to save money to go for fertility treatments." A sick feeling settled in the pit of her belly. "You don't think she planned on using the flashlight to blackmail the Faulkners, do you?"

"It sounds crazy," Duncan said.

"But if Missy is so desperate to have a baby, she might be desperate enough to think she could force them to pay her for the evidence that would keep Mark out of jail." Fiona spun away, shoving a hand through her hair. "This sounds crazy."

"There's only one way to find out if the theory holds merit," Duncan said. "Confront Missy..." he said, taking the file from Fiona, "with the file she used to break into the evidence locker."

Fiona nodded. "God, I hope she hasn't contacted the Faulkners with her prize yet. She doesn't know how dangerous they are. They won't give her the money she wants. They'll just take the flashlight."

Duncan's mouth set in a grim line. "And kill her."

CHAPTER 13

"Can you get the sheriff on his phone?" Duncan asked.

"I'll try," Fiona said, "He's liable to be in a dead zone for cell towers, if he's still on the road." She picked up the phone on the sheriff's desk and dialed Sheriff Barron's cell number. When he didn't respond, she said, "I'll try the radio in his service vehicle." She lifted the radio on his desk and clicked the button on the side. "Sheriff Barron, do you read me?"

Duncan leaned close to the radio and waited.

"This is the sheriff," a voice said, static making it difficult but not impossible to understand his response.

"Sheriff, when you get to a point you can call me on your cell phone, do it," Fiona said. "It's important."

"Will do." The radio when silent. Several minutes

179

later, Fiona's cell phone rang. She accepted the call, put it on speaker and started talking without preamble, "Sir, we know who took the flashlight from the evidence locker."

"Yeah? Who?" the sheriff responded.

"Missy Drennan," Fiona said.

A long silence ensued. For a moment, Duncan thought they'd lost connection with the sheriff.

"Are you sure?" he finally said.

"I think so," Fiona said. "It sounds crazy, but she was here that day it disappeared."

"Why didn't anyone mention it?" the sheriff asked.

"I don't know. She'd only come to deliver cookies that day."

"I remember the cookies," the sheriff said. "They were my favorite oatmeal raisin. Damn. Is Cole Drennan in on the theft?"

"We don't know," Fiona said. "We just figured it out."

"I'll be back in Eagle Rock in forty-five minutes. Let me confront Drennan. He's working the day shift, isn't he?"

"He is," Fiona said.

"Why would Missy take the evidence?" the sheriff asked.

"All we can think is that she might use it to blackmail the Faulkners for money."

"Damn dangerous," Sheriff Barron said. "They'll never let her get away with it."

"Our thoughts, too," Fiona said, her gaze meeting Duncan's.

"Fee, you can't let her go to the Faulkners," the sheriff said. "If she gives them the flashlight, we have nothing to pin Mark with Clay Bennett's murder. As it is, she might already have contaminated the evidence and destroyed the fingerprints."

"I'm more worried about what they'll do to Missy if she goes out there alone," Fiona said.

"You're right. They won't let her walk away after delivering the goods." The sheriff paused. "Find Missy. We can't let her get to the Faulkners."

"Yes, sir. Let us know when you get back. I'll have my radio on me."

"Will do. And Guthrie..."

"Yes, sir?"

"Be careful. I can't afford to lose all my deputies."

"Yes, sir." She ended the call and met Duncan's gaze. "We have to find Missy."

"Where should we look?" Duncan asked. "Where do they live?"

"Their house is here in town." Fiona looked through her contacts on her cellphone and touched the Drennans' home phone number.

After a couple of minutes, Fiona shook her head. "She's not answering."

"She could be outside in the yard," Duncan suggested.

"It's not far from here," Fiona said. "Let's go by."

Duncan followed Fiona to her SUV and climbed into the passenger seat.

Fiona slipped behind the steering wheel, cranked the engine and shifted into reverse.

While Fiona drove the few short blocks and turned onto a side street, Duncan scanned the sidewalks and the store windows, hoping to catch sight of Missy Drennan.

When they pulled in front of the little house the Drennans rented, he got out first and rounded the SUV.

Fiona climbed down from the vehicle and closed the door.

Duncan cupped his hand and peered through the little window in the front door. "No one appears to be home."

Fiona stepped up beside him and twisted the door handle. It opened easily, and the door swung inward. "Missy? Are you home?" she called out.

She stepped inside and looked around.

"Now who's breaking the law?" Duncan asked and stepped in behind her.

"We both are. But for a good reason," she said. "To help a friend."

They walked through the house checking all of the rooms, looking for Missy and the stolen evidence.

All of the rooms were neat and clean with nothing out of place. The last bedroom on the short hallway was only a little larger than a big closet. A twin bed took up one corner, a baby crib sat in the other. A wooden rocking chair stood between. The crib appeared to be made up with fresh sheets, a colorful mobile.

"She really was ready to have a baby," Fiona whispered.

"Isn't it a little soon for them to have all this set up? I mean, she's not even pregnant," Duncan said.

Fiona rubbed her arms, a chill slipping across her skin. "It's a bit obsessive, if you ask me. But then, they have been trying for a while."

"Any sign of the flashlight?" he asked.

"I didn't see anything," Fiona said.

"Where else might she be?"

Fiona shrugged. "Shopping or at the tavern or diner?"

"I didn't see her in any of the shops on Main Street. But then, I couldn't see inside all of them."

"We can start on Main Street, check in the diner and tavern."

"If all else fails, we'll contact her husband. He should know where his wife is," Duncan said.

Fiona's brow wrinkled. "I don't want him to know why we're looking for her."

Duncan nodded. "Understandable. Especially if he's in on the heist."

They had just returned to Fiona's vehicle when her service radio chirped. "Deputy Guthrie, report."

Fiona hit the mic, "Guthrie, here."

"Just received a distress call at the Iron Horse Ranch. You're needed there, ASAP. Just issued a BOLO on Missy Drennan."

Fiona's face blanched.

Duncan's heart sank to his knees.

"What happened?" Fiona said.

"Your baby is missing, and it appears Missy Drennan took her," Ellen said. "I'm so sorry, Fiona."

Duncan pulled his cellphone from his pocket and dialed home, placing the call on speaker.

His mother answered on the first ring. "Duncan. Oh, thank God. Have you heard?"

"We just did. What happened?"

"Missy came out looking for Fiona. We were having a nice visit in the living room with Caity playing on the floor." His mother sobbed.

"Take a deep breath, Mom."

He could hear her taking a shaky, sobbing breath before she continued. "Molly got up to go to the bathroom. Missy started coughing and asked for a drink of water. I asked Missy to keep an eye on Caity, and I went to the kitchen. When I got back..." His mother paused. "They were gone. Missy...the baby...gone."

"Mom. It's going to be all right. Breathe." Duncan prayed everything would be all right.

"Molly came out of the bathroom, and we ran to

the door. Missy was gone. Her car was gone. Caity was gone.

"Molly jumped in her Jeep and raced after Missy. I called 911 and... I'm so sorry. I never thought Missy would take Caity."

"How long ago did this happen?" Duncan asked.

"Maybe ten minutes ago?" his mother said. "She can't have gotten far."

"We're on our way out there. Hopefully, we'll see her on our way," Duncan said.

Fiona shifted into gear and pulled out onto the street. Her foot hit the accelerator hard, shooting them forward.

Duncan gripped the armrest without saying a word. Their daughter was in danger. They had to find Missy and Caity.

At the corner of the street, Fiona barely slowed, the backend of her SUV sliding sideways on loose gravel. Then they were on the highway blasting out of Eagle Rock toward Iron Horse Ranch.

"She has to be all right," Fiona murmured. She gripped the steering wheel so tightly her knuckles were as white as her face.

"She'll be okay. We have to believe that," Duncan said, his focus on the road ahead. "What kind of vehicle does Missy drive?"

"I think she drives a small, red compact car."

Duncan scanned the road ahead. He even looked in the ditches, hating the thought of Missy having an accident with Caity in the car. Caity wouldn't be in a child's car seat. If they crashed…

He couldn't think of that. They would find Missy, and Caity would be fine. He loved his little girl and wanted to spend his lifetime getting to know her.

Three miles out of town, they rounded a curve, and Fiona slammed on the brakes.

Duncan's shoulder strap tightened, keeping him from slamming his forehead into the dash.

A woman staggered toward them, her face ravaged by tears, her knees scraped, and her face bruised.

"Dear Lord," Fiona whispered. "That's Missy."

She ground to a halt in front of Missy and jumped out of the SUV.

Behind Missy, a Jeep slid to a halt on the shoulder, and Molly leaped out.

Duncan, Fiona and Molly converged on the woman.

First to her, Fiona gripped her arms and demanded. "Where's Caity?"

Missy stared at her through tear-filled eyes. "I only wanted to take her to my home to play in the baby's room. I wasn't going to hurt her."

Fiona lowered her voice and spoke softly, insistently. "Where is she?"

Missy looked into Fiona's face, her eyes clearing as if she just recognized who was in front of her. "Oh, Fiona, I'm so sorry. They took her. They took her and demanded you be the one to make the trade. You have to give it to them. They'll only accept it from you. And you have to go alone."

Duncan's chest tightened. He almost wished he didn't know what she was talking about, but he did. If they hadn't pieced together the case of the missing flashlight, he might have been confused by Missy's garbled message. But he wasn't. He knew who had his daughter and what it would take to get her back.

Fiona let go of Missy's arms and let her own drop to her sides. She felt as if someone had stabbed her in the gut and twisted the knife.

Molly spun Missy around and shook her slightly "What are you talking about? Where's Caity. Tell me now." Her eyes filled with tears that ran down her cheeks. "I was only out of the room for a few minutes. Tell me."

Duncan touched his sister's shoulder. "We know."

Molly looked at her brother through watery eyes. "Where?"

"The Faulkners have her," Fiona said, her tone as flat as she felt. Those animals had her daughter. She could almost feel the fear her daughter must be experiencing, and it broke her heart in two.

Duncan took Missy's hands and held them gently, staring into her face with a fierce intensity. "Missy, where is the flashlight?"

"I hid it. I wasn't going to give it to them. I changed my mind." Missy shook her head, her eyes glassy, looking into Duncan's but not seeing him. "I hid it where no one would find it until I could return it to the department."

"Where did you hide it," Duncan asked, keeping his voice steady and gentle.

Her eyes widened and filled with tears. "Duncan, I didn't mean to hurt Caity. You have to know that. I wouldn't hurt her for the world."

"I know that," he said. "But focus, Missy. We have to get that flashlight."

Missy shook her head and looked down at his chest. "I hid it."

"Where."

"In the woods."

"What woods?" Fiona asked, barely managing not to scream at the woman.

Missy turned her head toward Fiona. "In the woods behind my house."

Duncan squeezed Missy's hand. "You need to come with us to help us find it."

Missy let Duncan lead her toward the car. When he opened the door for her to get in, she planted her feet in the gravel and refused to get inside. "Only Fiona can take the flashlight to them. They said they'd shoot anyone else."

Duncan nodded. "Fiona will be the one to take it," he assured her.

Fiona followed, her heart numb, her mind spinning through all the facts so fast she felt as if it were short-circuiting.

Missy finally got into the backseat of Fiona's SUV.

"Molly, get in with Missy," Duncan said. "Make sure she stays."

Molly nodded and slid into the backseat beside Missy then slipped an arm around the woman, appearing to comfort her, when she was more likely holding her to keep her from trying to throw herself from the vehicle.

When Fiona started around to the driver's side, Duncan beat her to it. "I'll drive. You call the sheriff and let him know what's happening. And it's time to get Cole Drennan involved."

Fiona hurried around to the passenger side and slid in. She was on the radio to the sheriff before she buckled her seatbelt. She had to keep moving, keep pushing, keep praying that everything would be all right.

Duncan turned the SUV around and headed back to Missy's house.

Fiona contacted dispatch and had Ellen relay a message to Cole Drennan to have him meet them at his home.

Duncan pulled out his cellphone and handed it to Fiona. "Find Hank Patterson's number."

She searched through his contacts until she found

the one she wanted. As soon as there was enough cellphone reception, she dialed the number and handed the phone to Duncan.

About that time, they turned onto the Drennans' street.

Cole was there when they pulled up in front of the house. He met them at the SUV.

Fiona climbed out, leaving Duncan inside, talking to his friend Hank.

"What's wrong?" Cole asked, and turned as white as a sheet when Molly helped Missy out of the backseat.

Duncan came out of the house and joined them by the SUV

"Missy, sweetheart, what happened? Oh, sweet girl, let me see." He tipped her head up and stared at the bruising on her cheekbone and the eye that was just starting to swell shut. "Who did this to you?" He looked to Fiona and Duncan.

"The Faulkners," Fiona said.

"What they did was wrong, but right now, you can't go off half-cocked. They have Caity," Duncan said. "They want what Missy took from the evidence locker."

Cole's brow furrowed. "I don't understand."

Missy burst into tears and buried her face in her husband's uniform. "I took it. I took the flashlight."

Cole set her at arm's length, his jaw tight. "Why?"

"I thought they would pay me to give it to them."

She shook her head. "I knew it was wrong, but I did it anyway. I wanted the money. We need it for our plans."

"Oh, Missy. You can't start a family on tainted money." He pulled her close and held her.

"I know. And I'm sorry. I was going to put it back, but it was too late. I'd already let them know I had it." She pushed back and looked up into Cole's eyes. "I hid it where they wouldn't find it until I could put it back. I swear. I was going to put it back."

"I believe you, sweetheart. I believe you."

"But now, they have Caity. I wanted her to see our baby room. I wanted to see how our baby room would look with a baby in it. I wasn't going to keep her."

"You took Caity?" Cole pinched the bridge of his nose. "Where is she?"

"They took her from me. They ran me off the road and hit me. Then they took Caity." Missy burst into tears and sobbed so hard, she could barely breathe.

"Cole." Fiona touched his arm. "Missy has to show us where to find the flashlight. The Faulkners are demanding it in exchange for Caity. Missy said she hid it in the woods."

Cole nodded and looked down at his wife, his face ragged and gray, seeming to have aged ten years. "Missy, show me where you hid the flashlight."

She struggled to wrap her arms around him.

Cole held her at bay. "You have to show us where you hid it."

"I can't," she cried.

"Yes. You can," he said. "I'll help you. Come on." He took her hand and led her around the house. Their yard backed up to a forest of pine and fir trees.

Fiona would have run into the woods if she thought it would do any good. But Missy was the only person who knew where she'd hidden it.

"Which way did you go?" Cole asked.

"Along the trail you and I walk when we go for picnics," she said and sniffed. She rubbed her eyes with the heels of her palms and blinked several times before setting off into the woods with Cole.

"Remember how we had a picnic in the meadow...?" she asked as she walked.

Duncan took Fiona's hand and held her back a few steps.

She wanted to shout at Missy to hurry. They didn't have time for her to walk down memory lane. Caity's life hung in the balance. She had to be crying by now. The Faulkners wouldn't be patient with a crying baby.

Missy kept walking, her focus on the trail in front of her.

"I remember the picnic," Cole said softly. "Did you hide it in the meadow?"

She shook her head. "No. It would be too easy to find in the meadow."

Fiona swallowed hard on a sob rising up her throat. Did Missy even know where she'd hidden the flashlight? Or had she lost her mind and couldn't remember?

Duncan slid an arm around Fiona's waist and pulled her close as they walked. "She's going to be okay," he whispered.

"I hope the hell you're right," Molly said from behind him.

Fiona's thoughts echoed Molly's words.

Missy walked further into the woods until Fiona was almost certain the woman had no idea where she'd left the flashlight.

About the time Fiona was ready to turn back and take her chances by showing up at the Faulkner place empty-handed, Missy stopped at a dead tree next to the trail. The tree appeared to be hollow, the center having rotted out over the years.

Missy reached into the hollow and pulled out what looked like a black fifty-five-gallon garbage bag tightly wrapped around a narrow cylinder the size of the heavy-duty flashlight Mark Faulkner had used to beat Clay Bennett to death.

Fiona nearly fainted with relief.

Cole took the package from Missy and handed it to Fiona. "I'm sorry this happened. I knew she was suffering, but I didn't realize just how much. I'd go with you to help you recover Caity, but—"

"You need to stay with Missy," Fiona touched her coworker's arm. "Thank you."

Then she turned and ran back down the path as fast as her legs could carry her.

Duncan ran close behind her, his gait uneven, his bad leg probably causing him pain.

She couldn't slow and wait for him. Caity needed her. When they emerged into the Drennans' backyard, Duncan grabbed her arm and pulled her to a halt. "Fiona, you can't just race out there without a plan."

"They have Caity. Do you have any idea of how scared she'll be?" Fiona jerked free of his grip.

"Yes. But going off half-cocked won't save her or you. I've got a plan. But you have to listen and be ready for it."

"I can't let them hurt my baby," Fiona said, tears welling in her eyes. "Caity won't understand what's happening. She doesn't know those people. She'll cry. And they'll...they'll..." She turned and ran toward her SUV.

Again, Duncan caught up to her as she ripped open the driver's side door. Again, he caught her arm. "Listen, Fee. Once they get that evidence, there's nothing to stop them from killing you and Caity. That sounds harsh, but you have to hear it. I have a plan, but you have to be a part of it, or we lose everything, including Caity."

The pressure on her arm and the intensity in his

gaze finally got through to her. Her mind stilled. "Okay, I'm listening, but you need to make it quick."

He smiled briefly. "My friend, Hank Patterson, is on his way out toward the Faulkners with several of his men. I'm not sure how many, but they're highly trained in combat. Former SEALs, Rangers, Delta Force."

Fiona shook her head. "Missy said I had to go alone or they'll kill Caity."

Duncan nodded. "I know. These men know how to infiltrate without being seen or heard. They can get close enough to even the odds and ensure that when you make the trade, they don't shoot you anyway." He stared down into her eyes. "I want Caity back as much as you do. But I don't want to lose you in the process. And if they kill you, what are the chances Caity will make it out of there alive?"

Every instinct told Fiona to *go, go, go!* But Duncan was right. Once the Faulkners had what they wanted, they'd kill her and hide the body where no one could find it. And Caity…

Her fists clenched. She would not die and leave Caity to whatever horrible fate the Faulkners had in mind. "Okay, Duncan, what's the plan?"

CHAPTER 14

Duncan, Hank Patterson and every man Hank could pull from his band of Brotherhood Protectors met on the highway just past the turnoff for the dirt road leading to the Faulkner compound.

Dusk had bled into darkness, giving them the concealment they'd need to sneak in.

With eight of Hank's men, Sheriff Barron and four deputies, Duncan, Angus, Colin, Sebastian and Molly, they had almost as many people ready to move on the compound as the Faulkners had inside.

The Faulkners had the home field advantage of knowing the lay of the land and holding the hostage. One wrong move, and they wouldn't hesitate to kill Caity and Fiona. At that point, it would be an all-out war. Duncan clenched his fists. He'd kill anyone who dared to harm the two people he loved most.

Thankfully, he'd been able to get through to Fiona

to keep her from running right into their trap. She'd given Hank's team, the McKinnons and the deputies just enough time to assemble and start their trek through the woods to get in position for when she arrived to make the trade.

The Brotherhood Protectors and the McKinnons would take the lead, having had the most experience in combat and extractions.

Hank had brought the latest in communications devices and had equipped Fiona with a two-way radio earbud. She was able to easily hide it by letting her hair hang down over her ears.

The military men eased through the forest, staying low and quiet, moving quickly to get into place before Fiona turned onto the road and drove up to the compound in her SUV.

When they were close enough they could see people moving around the buildings, Duncan talked to Fiona. "Ready?"

"Yes. The sooner I get to Caity, the better."

"Just remember, when you make the exchange, take Caity and go. We'll be ready to move in immediately."

"Got it. I'm on the dirt road now, almost there," she said. "I'll go silent once I stop."

"I'm here, and I'll hear everything you say. If you think anything is important, repeat it so we'll know what they're saying, too. But don't be too obvious."

"Okay," she said.

"And, Fiona, we still haven't had our talk. But you should know…I love you, and I'll do everything in my power to get you and Caity out of there alive." He knew the entire team, his brothers and the sheriff's crew could hear his words, but he wanted them to. He wanted everyone to know just how much Fiona and Caity meant to him. "You're my world, and I don't want to live without you."

"I love you, too," Fiona whispered.

A moment later, she announced, "I'm here."

Duncan's heart stopped beating for a long second, and then raced ahead. This was it. The most important combat operation of his life.

Hank had sent some of his men to the far side of camp to give him an idea of how many men were standing guard on the perimeter.

Swede and Bear had swung north, Swede stopping at the north end, Bear moving on to the west side.

Duke and Taz went south, Taz taking the southeastern quadrant, Duke moving on to the southwest.

"What have we got?" Hank whispered into his headset.

"North end has one bogey ten yards into the woods, picking his nose," Swede reported.

"West side backs up to the mountain. All clear. Going closer," Bear said.

"Southeast, one bogey leaning on the fender of a

dual axle pickup, armed with an AR-15. I can take him," Taz said. "He's focusing on the road in."

"Southwest is clear, moving closer," Duke reported.

Duncan's oldest brother, Angus, a seasoned Delta Force operative, had slipped through the darkest shadows, coming to within twenty yards of the south side of the road leading into the compound. "I've got one bogey in sight, south side of the road. Fifteen feet from my position."

Sebastian, Duncan's other brother who'd been with the Navy SEALs for the past seven years reported softly, "North of entry road, one bogey, eight yards from my position."

Hank gave the order, "All others, move in to position and wait for the exchange. Our goal is not to kill, but to disable their ability to harm Deputy Guthrie and the baby."

Duncan crept through the shadows until he was positioned at the edge of the clearing, the closest he could get to where Fiona had parked her SUV.

She was just opening the door and getting out with her hands held high in the air. "I'm not armed, and I'm alone."

"You better be. The kid's life depends on it," Barb Faulkner called out from where she stood on the porch.

Duncan could hear a baby whimpering, but he

couldn't see Caity from where he lay low in the underbrush.

"I brought the flashlight," Fiona said.

"Bring it to us," Beau Faulkner demanded from where he stood beside his mother.

Fiona shook her head. "Not until I get my baby."

"Seems you'll do whatever we tell you to." Tripp Faulkner stepped out of the shadows of one of the smaller buildings near the cabin. "You don't have much of a choice."

"I came in good faith," Fiona said. "I came for my daughter. She has done nothing to deserve being used as a bargaining chip."

"Yeah, but she makes a good one, doesn't she?" Mark Faulkner stepped out of the log cabin, carrying Caity in his arms.

Duncan's fists clenched. From where he lay in the shadows, he could see Fiona stiffen.

"I'm reaching into my vehicle for the flashlight," Fiona announced and bent slowly to grab the black trash bag wrapped tightly around the flashlight Mark had used as a murder weapon.

She straightened, still standing in the door of the vehicle and held up the evidence that could put Mark behind bars for the rest of his life. "I'll give it to you, when you give me Caity," Fiona said.

"How do we know you brought the real thing?" Mark asked. "Unwrap it."

"It's the real thing," she assured him. She tore at

the thin black plastic and then the brown paper the item had been wrapped in to preserve the fingerprints. When she had it all ripped away, she held up the flashlight. "It has a bent shaft. The same one we found near Clay's body in that ditch off the highway."

"Wouldn't have ruined my good flashlight if Bennett had died after the first couple of swings," Mark muttered. "The bastard wasn't cooperating."

Fiona snorted. "I don't know too many people who want to just lay down and die."

"Yeah, well, even Beau had to take a crack at him to keep him down," Mark admitted.

"What? You weren't man enough to do the job yourself?" Fiona jabbed.

Duncan bunched his muscles and brought his legs up beneath him. The Faulkners had just admitted they'd killed Clay Bennett. They wouldn't have done that to a sheriff's deputy if they planned on letting her get away. They were going to kill Fiona.

"I'm more man than you'll ever know," Mark said.

"That was pretty sloppy of you to leave the murder weapon with the body," Fiona said.

"I didn't," Mark said. He shot a heated look at Beau. "That was Beau's doing."

"And we all know Wally Bing's murder weapon was that truck." Fiona nodded toward the jacked-up truck. "The dent in the fender tells it all."

"Maybe I'll run you over like I ran over Bing," Tripp said.

"Shut up, you fools," Barb said. "You talk too damn much. Get the flashlight and be done with it."

Fiona lifted her chin. "If you want the flashlight, you'll have to come get it, and bring Caity with you." She held the flashlight up in the air. Her body blocked by the door of the SUV.

Mark stepped down from the porch and walked across the clearing toward the SUV.

When Caity saw her mother standing a few steps away, she cried and held out her arms, wiggling so much Mark nearly dropped her.

"Damn kid," he cursed. "Be still." He stopped a few feet away from Fiona's car. "You'll have to come get her, if you want her. And you better hurry before I drop the brat."

Fiona hesitated. "I'm coming," she said and stepped out of the relative protection of her SUV door into the open.

She walked toward Mark and stopped in front of him. "Give me my daughter."

Caity threw herself toward Fiona.

Fiona tossed the flashlight on the ground and grabbed for the baby. As soon as she had her in her arms, she spun and hurried toward her car door.

"Go, go, go," Duncan said softly. If she made it to the SUV, they had a chance of getting away without being caught in any crossfire.

She had just about reached the door when Tripp Faulkner put out an arm, blocking her path. "You didn't really think we'd let you go, did you?"

"If you know what's good for you, you'll get out of my way," Fiona said, her tone low and threatening.

"You know how much we can get for a kid on the black market?" Beau asked, stepping down from the porch. "I bet we can get ten grand for that brat. They like little girls."

Duncan's stomach roiled. He'd be damned if those bastards laid one more hand on his little girl. This party had to come to an end. It might as well be now. "I'm coming, Fiona," he said into his headset.

"It's okay, Caity. Mama's got you now. Everything's going to be fine." Fiona had almost made it back to her SUV. She could see her escape only a few short feet ahead. All she had to do was get herself and Caity past Tripp, and she'd be on her way home.

But the distance might as well have been a continent away. As Duncan and the others had suspected, the Faulkners weren't going to let her walk away. Not knowing what she knew.

They'd blatantly admitted to killing Clay Bennett and Wally Bing. Fiona would not be allowed to leave on her own two feet. They'd be carrying her out in the bed of one of their pickups to dump along the side of the road, much as they'd dumped the body of Clay Bennett. And the Faulkners would get away with yet another murder and the subsequent kidnapping and sale of a baby on the black market.

Fiona stiffened. She refused to let them touch Caity ever again. She'd protect her daughter with her life. Sweet Jesus, where was the cavalry? Why hadn't they already come to the rescue?

Then she heard Duncan's voice in her ear. "I'm coming, Fiona."

She held her breath, hugged Caity close to her and searched the surrounding area. Caity clung to her, her diaper heavy and needing to be changed, her eyes moist from tears. Poor baby. She'd been through so much. And the trouble wasn't over yet.

"Give me the kid," Tripp said and reached out to take Caity from Fiona's arms.

She turned away from him, refusing to give up Caity.

"Bitch, give me the kid," he demanded.

Fiona waited until he got close enough and reached around her for Caity.

She bit his arm and stomped hard on his instep.

Tripp jerked back his arm and hopped on his good foot. "Bitch. You'll pay for that." He cocked his arm, his fist clenched.

"You want to hit someone, why not pick on someone your own size," a voice said from the edge of the clearing and in her ear.

Duncan stepped out into the open, his gun drawn and aimed at Tripp's chest, and his eyes narrowed.

"Or do you only pick on women because you're not man enough to handle anyone stronger?"

"You should have stayed out of this, McKinnon," Barb said from on the porch. "You're in Faulkner territory, not on Iron Horse Ranch."

"I might be on Faulkner land, but I'm also in the great state of Montana where it's illegal to murder people and steal babies. Your sons belong in jail."

Barb crossed her arms over her chest. "My family stands together. You have a problem with one of us, you have a problem with all of us."

"Then that would make you guilty as an accessory to murder or at least for obstruction of justice," Duncan said. "And my family stands together as well. Fiona and Caity are part of my family, and we don't take kindly to people who hurt members of our family or threaten them."

"And what are you going to do about it?" Barb asked. "You appear to be outnumbered. What's to keep us from killing you and dumping your body in one of the canyons?"

"Family is what will keep you from killing our brother," Angus said, stepping out of the shadows with one of the sentries in his grasp, a sock in his mouth and his wrists zip-tied behind his back. Angus held a gun pointed at Beau Faulkner.

"You think just because you were some hotshot in the military you can take down every last one of us?" Mark snorted. "You must have rocks for brains."

"Or more brothers to stand up for family." Colin pushed a man in front of him, similarly bound and gagged as the one Angus had standing in between him and the Faulkners.

"McKinnons stand for each other," Sebastian said, nudging yet another of the Faulkner clan out into the open.

"You're damn right we do," Molly said, shoving her Faulkner catch in front of her. "We all heard you admit you killed Clay Bennett and Wally Bing. We have enough witnesses to testify that we won't need the flashlight to convict Mark and Beau for murder."

"It'll be Faulkners' word against McKinnons. And everyone knows the families don't get along," Barb growled.

"Think again." Sheriff Barron walked out into the open, his weapon drawn. "Everyone, put your weapons down. Mark, Tripp and Beau Faulkner, you're under arrest for murder. Barb, you're under arrest for kidnapping and aggravated assault."

"You won't be taking me anywhere," Tripp said. He lunged for Fiona.

Fiona, clutching Caity to her breast, dodged Tripp's grasp.

A shot rang out.

Tripp fell to the ground at Fiona's feet and lay moaning.

When Fiona turned back to the clearing, she fully expected an all-out war to have begun.

The Faulkner men stood still, their hands on their guns, but none of them drawn.

Hank's men had stepped out of the woods, along with the deputies in uniform.

Fiona's heart filled with hope,

"Who wants to be next?" the sheriff called out.

Duncan crossed to Fiona and stood between her and the Faulkners.

No one spoke.

Barb's eyes narrowed. "You gonna help my boy, or let him bleed to death?"

"Now, that's up to you," the sheriff said. "When your people lay down their guns, we'll check on your son."

Barb nodded. "Put 'em down, boys."

When no one moved to follow her orders, she barked, "Now!"

Rifles, shotguns and handguns hit the dirt.

"And the knives," Sheriff Barron said.

"You heard the sheriff," Barb grumbled.

Knives dropped to the ground.

"You, too, Mrs. Faulkner." Sheriff Barron nodded toward her. "I know you keep a pistol strapped to your leg. It goes, too."

She leaned down, lifted her pantleg, pulled a small handgun from a leather holster strapped to her ankle and tossed it onto the ground.

Sheriff Barron turned to one of the deputies. "Bring in the ambulance."

Moments later, the sound of an ambulance's siren wailed not far from where they were. A few minutes later, it bumped up the rutted road to the compound.

EMTs leaped out. One examined Caity. The other bent to work on Tripp.

Fiona wished Tripp would die. She didn't like that she felt that way, but after he'd threatened to take her child and sell her on the black market, the man deserved a slow painful death.

Duncan stood by her as the EMT took Caity's vitals and found a diaper in one of the storage cabinets in the ambulance.

Fiona changed her daughter and brushed her dark hair away from her face.

When she was dry and more comfortable, she lay against Fiona's chest, her body shaking with hiccups from having cried so much.

Anger burned inside Fiona. Anyone who could take a baby away from her family and use her as a pawn in a deadly game wasn't human.

While Hank and his men stood guard over the Faulkner clan, the deputies hurried back to where they'd parked their cars on the highway and came back to collect Mark, Beau and Barb, tucking them into the back of different vehicles to be transported to the jail in Eagle Rock. They'd be transferred to the state prison the following day. Tripp was loaded into an ambulance and taken to the nearest hospital.

The sheriff processed half a dozen more of the

men in the Faulkner compound for outstanding warrants. His deputies would be busy transporting them to the jail.

Fiona didn't care. Caity needed to be fed and bathed to get the stench of the Faulkners off her skin.

Duncan slipped his arm around her and pulled her into the strength of his big body. "Ready to go home?"

She nodded and let him lead her to the SUV.

Caity cried when she tried to put her into her car seat.

"Oh, sweetie, everything's going to be all right, now. The bad people won't ever hurt you, again. Mama and Daddy will take good care of you." She strapped Caity in, her heart squeezing hard in her chest as Caity reached out, wanting Fiona to hold her.

"Ride in the back with Caity," Duncan said. "I'll drive."

Fiona slid into the backseat with her baby and draped her arm over the child.

Caity wrapped her little arms around Fiona's hand and pulled it up to her cheek. She cried and fussed a little as they bumped along the rutted road out to the highway. Once they were on a smooth road, the baby drifted off to sleep, waking every so often to look for her mother.

Fiona fought tears all the way home. She wondered how long it would take for Caity to recover from the trauma of being taken away from the people she knew and loved. Would she have nightmares about the bad people who'd stolen her away?

Fiona would do everything in her power to make her baby feel safe again. And she'd do whatever she could to ensure her daughter would grow up knowing what a brave father she had. A man who would risk his life to save her and her mother from murderers and thieves.

"You two all right back there?" Duncan asked as they drove through the stone and wrought iron gate of the Iron Horse Ranch.

Fiona felt a huge sense of relief as they passed through the gate and continued to the ranch house.

To her, this was the closest she'd felt to coming home in a very long time. She hoped and prayed that what Duncan had said right before she'd gone in to make the exchange for Caity were words he meant, that he really did love her. Because she loved him with all of her heart and couldn't imagine going through the rest of her life without him.

CHAPTER 15

DUNCAN STAYED with Fiona and Caity throughout the night. They'd laid Caity on the bed between them until she'd fallen asleep, and then moved her to her crib.

He held Fiona in his arms, happy they'd survived the whole ordeal with the Faulkners without anyone but Tripp sustaining a wound.

Caity woke a couple of times during the night, crying for her mother.

Each time, Fiona held her in the rocking chair until the little girl settled down and finally slept until morning.

When Caity woke in the morning, Duncan took her downstairs to let Fiona rest. With his mother's help, he fed her a bottle of formula and some baby cereal and played with her on the floor.

The child was nothing if not resilient. She smiled

and played as though she hadn't been kidnapped and nearly killed the day before.

"How's she doing?" Duncan's mother came to sit on the floor with Duncan and smiled at Caity. "I'm so sorry about what happened yesterday. It was all my fault. I never should have left Caity alone with Missy."

"You couldn't have known," a voice said from behind Duncan.

He turned to find Fiona dressed in a pale-yellow sundress and white sandals, her glorious red hair freshly washed, dried and hanging in soft waves down around her shoulders. She was the most beautiful woman he'd ever known. And brave. She'd gone into the lion's den to rescue her baby and had come out the victor.

Duncan held out his hand to her.

She dropped to her knees beside him on the rug and smiled at his mother. "Caity's going to be fine."

As if to prove it, Caity held out a toy to her grandmother as if to invite her to play.

Tears welled in Duncan's mother's eyes. "I love this child so much. I don't know what I would have done if…"

"It's over," Fiona said. "If I had been here yesterday when Missy had come to visit, I probably would've done the same thing. There was no reason to believe she'd take off with Caity. She'd never done anything like that before."

Duncan's mother wiped at a tear and nodded. "I hope someday you'll trust me to keep her sometimes. I miss having a baby around this big old house."

"I trust you, now," Fiona assured her. "I'm so glad Caity has a grandmother to love and who loves her."

"I had a call this morning from Cole Drennan," Duncan's mother said softly. "He called to check on Caity and Fiona. He apologized for what Missy did and said he was getting her the best help he could find. He loves her so much. You know they've been trying to get pregnant for years, and when she miscarried her last pregnancy, she had a nervous breakdown. She's going to see someone about getting on antidepressants. And he thought about getting her a puppy to keep her company. Something she could love and care for while she's working on getting better."

"I feel so bad for her." Fiona shook her head. "I can't imagine not being able to have a baby. I feel very lucky to have had Caity, and I would do anything for her."

"And so would I. Anytime you want me to watch her, I'm there." Duncan's mother pushed to her feet. "Now, I need to figure out what I'm going to make for lunch. You haven't even had breakfast. Can I get you anything?"

Fiona shook her head. "I'll just wait and eat something at lunch. Thank you."

Once his mother was out of earshot, Duncan faced Fiona.

And she faced him.

"We need to talk," he said at the same time she did.

He laughed and reached for her hand. "Yes, we do." Now that they were going to have that conversation, he wasn't sure exactly what he could say to convince her that he loved her, and not just because she was the mother of his baby.

"Fiona, I meant what I said when you were going into the Faulkner compound."

"You said a lot of things." She laced her fingers through his. "Can you be more specific? Because, if you can't, I can go first."

"No, I need to say this," he said bringing her hand up to his lips where he pressed a kiss to the backs of her knuckles. "Growing up, you were always there. My best friend, my buddy and my sidekick. I could count on you for anything, including giving me advice on the poor decisions I made in the girls I dated."

She nodded, her lips twitching into a smile. "You didn't always choose well."

"No, I didn't. And I think it was because I didn't need any of them, and I chose girls who weren't right for me because I had the right one already, and I didn't know it." His lifted his chin and gazed into her eyes. "I think I've always loved you, but I didn't realize that was what it was until the night fifteen months ago when we conceived Caity." He turned to smile at the baby trying to pull her knees under her to crawl.

"You had a funny way of showing me that you loved me," Fiona said, dropping her focus to their joined hands. "I didn't hear from you until you came home fifteen months later."

He nodded. "I'm not the smartest guy. I went back to a thirteen-month deployment to the hills of Afghanistan. I thought you would write to me like you always had. When you didn't, I figured you didn't feel the same way I did. I'd screwed up our friendship, and I regretted that the most."

"I was busy working and being pregnant and missing you. I thought you'd sobered up and realized you'd made a big mistake. I didn't tell you about the baby, hoping you'd call me, write to me, or anything, to tell me how you really felt. When you didn't, too much time had passed. I knew you were deployed, and I didn't want you to lose focus on your missions. I wanted you to come home alive." This time she lifted his hand and pressed her lips to his knuckles.

"I'm sorry. I wish I'd called the next day and all the days after." Duncan captured her hand in both of his. "Please, will you forgive me and give me a second chance to win your heart? Because, you see, I love you. I've always loved you, and I don't want to go another day without you in it."

She looked up, her gaze meeting his, her eyes

filling it tears. "You're not just saying that because of Caity?"

He shook his head. "I love Caity, and I'm so very glad she's a part of my life, but even if she hadn't been born of our union, I would have eventually figured out that I love you. All those months in the field, I looked for your letters. When they didn't come, I felt as if I'd lost the best part of me. My heart. I love you, Fiona Guthrie. And want you and Caity in my life. And when Caity is grown and moves out, I want to grow old with my best friend and the woman who makes me happy." He pulled her into his arms and kissed her. "The only one who makes me happy is you."

Fiona wrapped her arms around his neck and pressed her forehead to his. "You don't know how long I've waited to hear those words."

"Fiona," he said against her lips. "Will you marry me?"

She laughed and cried all at once. Then she whispered against his mouth, "I thought you'd never ask."

He leaned back, frowning. "That's not an answer."

She smiled and gave him the answer he'd been longing for. "Yes, Duncan McKinnon, Caity and I will marry you."

LATER THAT DAY

. . .

"What's this I hear about you and Fiona?" Angus asked as he climbed the porch stairs with his fiancée, Bree, on his arm.

"What did you hear?" Duncan tightened his arm around Fiona who sat beside him on the porch swing with Caity sleeping in her arms.

Bree smiled. "You're engaged?"

Fiona grinned. "We are."

Colin stepped out of the house. "About damn time, too. We all knew you and Fiona belonged together."

Duncan frowned. "You did?"

"Hell, yes." Sebastian followed Colin out of the house, carrying a couple bottles of beer. He handed one to Duncan. "She only had eyes for you, and you never could settle with any other female. It was obvious to everyone."

"Everyone but you," Angus said. "You must have taken too many knocks to the head, playing football."

Duncan nodded. "I must have. I had the best girl all along, and I was too thickheaded to realize it. But I have now, and she's agreed to marry me. I just need to get a ring to make it official."

"Speaking of rings," Molly said as she walked up from the direction of the barn. "I called the pawn shop Tripp mentioned in Bozeman. At first, they didn't remember it. When I sent them a picture, they recalled that a woman brought it in a couple of days ago."

"Did they say who she was?"

"She said her name was Trixie Samuels. She gave an address in Bozeman. I wrote it down. He wasn't really confident that she was telling the truth. She looked like she was strung out and needed the money for drugs."

"Did he describe her?" Duncan asked.

Molly nodded. "He said she was a bleached blond with dark eyes."

"That could be a lot of women," Colin said.

"He said when she held out her hand for the money, she had a tattoo of a unicorn on her wrist."

"Well that narrows it down, probably to one woman. We just have to find her."

Colin nodded. "I'll go into Bozeman tomorrow and check out that address."

Duncan's lips pressed together. "It's about time we had a break. Dad's out there. I just know it. And he's waiting for us to find him."

THE BILLIONAIRE
HUSBAND TEST

BILLIONAIRE ONLINE DATING SERVICE
BOOK #1

New York Times & USA Today
Bestselling Author

ELLE JAMES

THE BILLIONAIRE

Husband
Test
BILLIONAIRE ONLINE DATING SERVICE

ELLE JAMES
NEW YORK TIMES BESTSELLING AUTHOR

CHAPTER 1

"DON'T LEAVE love up to luck. With the help of my firm and heavily tested computer algorithms, you will have a ninety-nine point nine percent chance of finding your perfect match." The attractive young woman, wearing a soft gray business suit and standing in front of the white board, clicked a hand-held remote control. A picture of a couple embracing at sunset on a beach materialized on the white surface. "What do you think? Willing to give my program a shot?"

"I don't know." Frank Cooper Johnson sat at the conference table with the other members of the Billionaires Anonymous Club. "Am I the only one who thinks this is a bad idea?"

"Mr. Johnson—" Leslie Lamb began.

"Call him Coop. All his friends call him that." Maxwell Smithson grinned.

"For the sake of argument, give my friend Leslie the benefit of the doubt." Taggert Bronson rose to stand beside the presenter. "Think about it. Didn't we all make the same plans? Work hard, work smart, make our first million by thirty, start a family by thirty-five...We're all on track—only better–instead of millions, we made our billions by thirty." Tag pointed to Gage Tate. "How's that media empire going?" He nodded toward Sean O'Leary. "Your oil speculating has you sitting pretty, doesn't it, Sean? And Coop, you and I are making billions on our financial investments. Have any of you even thought about the next step in our plan? How many of you are even dating?"

Sean raised his hand. "I've been dating."

"The same girl more than once?" Tag asked.

"Using a computer to find a mate just doesn't seem right." Coop pushed back his chair and rose. "When I find the woman I want to marry, I'll do it the old-fashioned way."

Tag snorted. "And meet her at a bar?"

"Any of you have any luck lately going to a bar and not being slammed by the paparazzi?"

Gage sighed. "Though I hate to admit it, the man has a point. I can't step outside my condo without being hit by at least a dozen cameras, much less go to dinner with anyone without being bombarded."

Leslie smiled. "That's the beauty of BODS—"

"Seriously?" Sean shook his head. "BODS?"

The woman drew herself up to her full five-foot-three inches and stared down her nose at Sean. "Billionaire Online Dating Service—BODS. It's an acronym, so sue me. As I was saying, the beauty of the system is that the communication is all done anonymously. You meet real woman, not money-grubbing, limelight-seeking gold-diggers."

Gage frowned. "They won't know that we're loaded?"

"Financial status is not one of the questions we ask on the online data collection system. I perform a background check on each entrant and the computer does the matching."

Tag spread his hands. "Don't you love it? And the match is all based on your own personality profile." He dropped his hands when none of the others spoke. "What have you got to lose?"

Shaking his head, Coop grumbled, "Our dignity. Participation is admitting we're hopeless at finding a date."

Leslie shook her head. "Not at all. The program gives you a better chance of finding someone who truly fits the life-style of your dreams. Tell you what. As my first customers—"

Gage shot to his feet. "Whoa, wait a minute. First?" He stared across at Tag. "I thought you said this system was proven?"

"It is...on volunteers." Tag held up his hands. "Leslie hasn't yet charged for her services. Calm down."

Coop crossed his arms, ready for the meeting to be over. "I don't relish being someone's guinea pig."

"You aren't." Leslie sucked in a deep breath and let it out. "Tell you what, how about I let you use my service free? If you find the woman of your dreams, then you pay me what you think the experience was worth."

"Can't get fairer than that." Tag grinned. "Who wants to be first to sign up?"

"I think you should be." Cooper pinned Tag with a challenging stare.

"I'm already in the system and aiming for a date next Friday." Tag's eyes narrowed. "How about it, Coop? Or are you afraid?"

Hell yeah, Cooper was afraid. What kind of loser would the computer match him up with? Then again, he wouldn't admit to any of them that the idea of dating was worse than public speaking...and he hated public speaking. That's why he worked the financial market and stayed behind the scenes. He lived on his ranch, raised his horses quietly—no fanfare and no paparazzi as long as he didn't step out on a date. So far, the arrangement had been very lucrative with no distractions. Lonely, but lucrative, about summed up his life.

"Look, Leslie is in a situation no different than we

were when we started out." Tag continued, "Give her business a chance. One date. That's all she's asking."

"Fine," Cooper said. "Anything to get this meeting over with."

Leslie's face bloomed with a huge smile. "I'll take you in Tag's office, one at a time to enter your data and show you the ropes. The process won't take long and you'll have your match. You won't regret your decision. I promise."

Cooper was already regretting his agreement, and he hadn't even been matched yet.

EMMA JACOB'S cell phone vibrated, indicating a text message. Sitting at a stoplight, she glanced at the message and sighed.

Set an extra plate at dinner. The message was from her oldest brother, Ace. More than likely, the guest was another attempt at fixing her up with a man. For the past month, all four of her brothers had taken it upon themselves to find Emma a husband.

Great, that's all she needed, more husband candidates forced on her by the worst matchmakers ever in Jacobs family history. Granted, her four brothers meant well, but really? If she'd wanted another man in her life, she'd have gone out and chosen one herself.

Truth was she was happy just the way things

were. Well, almost. She'd have been much happier if the love of her life had lived long enough for them to be married, have children and grow old together. But that hadn't been in the cards. Not once Marcus was deployed, got hit by an improvised explosion device and died before being transported back to the states.

Her throat tightened and she twisted the diamond engagement ring on her finger. For two years, she'd been mourning his death. You'd think her brothers would let it be, instead of telling her she should get back in the saddle.

Emma slipped the ring from her finger and tucked it into her wallet. Maybe removing the ring would lead her brothers to think she was ready to move on, even if she wasn't. That and her trip to Dallas and a meeting with the one friend, Leslie Lamb, she'd made in her grieving group would set her plan in motion. Emma had a special favor to ask of her friend. One she hoped would solve all her problems with her brothers.

"You want what?" Leslie leaned across her desk an hour later, tapping her pen against the notepad she'd been scribbling on.

"I want you to set me up on a date with a man that will completely fail to impress my brothers." Emma ticked off on her fingers. "He has to be nice looking. That fact will throw off the boys. Preferably someone who makes his living sitting behind a desk." She'd pictured a pasty computer geek, but didn't want to be that crude in front of Leslie.

"Let me get this straight. You want this date to fail?" Leslie shook her head. "I'm building a business, not tearing it down. How will that look to the guy I'm setting you up with if I match him with someone totally wrong for his preferences?"

Emma sat back, frowning. "Hmm, sorry. That's pretty narrow-minded, thinking only of myself." She chewed on her lip for a moment. "I guess I could go find some other online dating service and play Russian roulette." She sat up. "I'm sorry, Leslie, the idea was stupid. Just forget I asked. I know how hard you've worked to put together the business plan and line up investors for your dating service. I wish you lots of luck." Emma gathered her purse and stood. "I have to get back to the ranch before feeding time."

"Wait." Leslie left her chair and rounded her desk, laying a hand on Emma's arm. "Do me a favor first and fill out a form on my computer. Be honest, don't fudge the data and let's see what happens."

Already shaking her head, Emma backed toward the door. "I don't want to set you up for failure. I'm really not interested in finding love. I had it."

Leslie squeezed her arm. "I know. Thinking of loving anyone else is hard, isn't it? I know exactly where you are. I haven't even tried, yet."

"Yet. At least you might some day." Emma shook

her head, pain pinching her throat. "Not me. I had the love of my life. I don't want second best."

"At least, give the system a chance to find a match that closely suits you. Give him one date, and maybe your brothers will get off your back."

"I don't know. I don't like leading someone on when I don't want it to go anywhere."

"Just do it and keep an open mind. We screen our clients and do background checks. At least, you know you won't be getting an ex-con or child molester. You won't regret it, I promise."

Emma chewed on her lip. Leslie's proposal might do the trick. She just didn't want her friend's match-making business to suffer the consequences. "The date is doomed to failure. Are you sure you want to take the hit?"

"Be honest with the data. The system will do the rest and I'm willing to take the risk."

For a long moment, Emma stared into her friend's hopeful face. "Anyone ever tell you saying no to you is hard?" She laughed. "If you keep that up, you should get lots of business."

Leslie nodded, a smug smile on her lips. "I plan on it. I only want others to have a chance at the love you and I have both known. I wouldn't have missed the experience for the world."

Emma sighed. "Me either." She let Leslie lead her into a spare office where she could use the computer to enter her data. Emma made a point of putting it all out there—the good, the bad and the not so attractive. If the system found someone to date her, the result would be a miracle. And once out at the ranch with her brothers running him through his paces, any prospect would soon learn no one would equal their expectations.

She'd be off the hook and free to pursue her own goals and dreams. Which included purchasing Old Man Rausch's one-hundred-and-fifty-acre spread on Willow Creek. The place would be all hers, paid for with the money she'd been saving from her work as a horse trainer for the T-Bar-M Ranch. Once she lived on her own, her brothers couldn't interfere with her life.

A good plan, and one she intended to see through.

As she stepped into her truck to make the long drive back to the Rockin' J Ranch, a cool breeze swept across the parking lot, lifting the hair off the back of her neck, surrounding her like a caress. She glanced at the sky. No clouds. Weird. The temperature read-out on the bank sign on the corner listed ninety-nine degrees. Heat waves rippled upward from the black pavement, and Emma had yet to switch on the truck AC. So where had the cool breeze come from? She could swear she smelled a faint hint of musky aftershave, the kind Marcus liked to wear when they'd gone out on dates.

Emma's chest tightened and she sat still, trying to recapture the scent. Finally, she gave up. She had to be imagining the smell. All this talk with Leslie about having loved the man of their dreams had played havoc with her memories. Nothing a good round of stall mucking wouldn't cure.

She'd never told anyone she thought Marcus's spirit lingered around her, keeping her company when she was lonely or afraid. Her brothers would have her in a shrink's office quicker than she could say *lickety-split*. At night, when she lay in bed, missing him so badly it hurt, a light breeze would stir the curtains and waft around her. She'd stare at the picture of them laughing on the beach at South Padre Island and sigh. Marcus was everything she'd ever wanted in life. With him gone, she didn't have anything to aim for, except the ranch and her independence.

If her plan to bring a "date" home to her brothers worked, she'd be one step closer to that independence she so craved and to quelling her brothers' determination to marry her off. The ball was in Leslie's court to find the right man to pull off the plan.

"Please be everything I asked for," Emma whispered as she cranked the truck engine. Another gentle breeze blew in through the open window and trailed across her skin, lifting more goose bumps. She shrugged and shifted into drive. Emma chastised herself for her morbid thoughts. If she didn't stop thinking every peculiar thing that happened in her life was a sign, she'd be forced to commit herself to the nearest psychiatric ward for evaluation.

ABOUT THE AUTHOR

ELLE JAMES also writing as MYLA JACKSON is a *New York Times* and *USA Today* Bestselling author of books including cowboys, intrigues and paranormal adventures that keep her readers on the edges of their seats. When she's not at her computer, she's traveling, snow skiing, boating, or riding her ATV, dreaming up new stories. Learn more about Elle James at www.ellejames.com

Website | Facebook | Twitter | GoodReads | Newsletter | BookBub | Amazon

Or visit her alter ego Myla Jackson at mylajackson.com
Website | Facebook | Twitter | Newsletter

Follow Me!
www.ellejames.com
ellejames@ellejames.com

Iron Horse Legacy

Soldier's Duty (#1)

Ranger's Baby (#2)

Marine's Promise (#3)

SEAL's Vow (#4)

Brotherhood Protectors Series

Montana SEAL (#1)

Bride Protector SEAL (#2)

Montana D-Force (#3)

Cowboy D-Force (#4)

Montana Ranger (#5)

Montana Dog Soldier (#6)

Montana SEAL Daddy (#7)

Montana Ranger's Wedding Vow (#8)

Montana SEAL Undercover Daddy (#9)

Cape Cod SEAL Rescue (#10)

Montana SEAL Friendly Fire (#11)

Montana SEAL's Mail-Order Bride (#12)

Montana Rescue (Sleeper SEAL)

Hot SEAL Salty Dog (SEALs in Paradise)

Hot SEAL Hawaiian Nights (SEALs in Paradise)

Brotherhood Protectors Vol 1

Hellfire Series

Hellfire, Texas (#1)

Justice Burning (#2)

Smoldering Desire (#3)

Hellfire in High Heels (#4)

Playing With Fire (#5)

Up in Flames (#6)

Total Meltdown (#7)

Declan's Defenders

Marine Force Recon (#1)

Show of Force (#2)

Full Force (#3)

Driving Force (#4)

Mission: Six

One Intrepid SEAL

Two Dauntless Hearts

Three Courageous Words

Four Relentless Days

Five Ways to Surrender

Six Minutes to Midnight

Hot Combat (#1)

Hot Target (#2)

Hot Zone (#3)

Hot Velocity (#4)

Cajun Magic Mystery Series

Voodoo on the Bayou (#1)

Voodoo for Two (#2)

Deja Voodoo (#3)

Cajun Magic Mysteries Books 1-3

Billionaire Online Dating Service

The Billionaire Husband Test (#1)

The Billionaire Cinderella Test (#2)

The Billionaire Bride Test (#3)

The Billionaire Daddy Test (#4)

The Billionaire Matchmaker's Test (#5)

SEAL Of My Own

Navy SEAL Survival

Navy SEAL Captive

Navy SEAL To Die For

Navy SEAL Six Pack

Devil's Shroud Series

Deadly Reckoning (#1)

Heir to Murder

Secret Service Rescue

High Octane Heroes

Haunted

Engaged with the Boss

Cowboy Brigade

Time Raiders: The Whisper

Bundle of Trouble

Killer Body

Operation XOXO

An Unexpected Clue

Baby Bling

Under Suspicion, With Child

Texas-Size Secrets

Cowboy Sanctuary

Lakota Baby

Dakota Meltdown

Beneath the Texas Moon